STATESIDE

LORI BEASLEY BRADLEY

Rowdy Waters stood outside The Devil's Den, hesitant to go inside the noisy bar where the pulsing beat of Give Me Two Steps vibrated the glass in the door. Since being discharged and returning from Afghanistan, he hadn't ventured out into the world much. He'd seen too much and lost too much.

His therapist at the VA Hospital told him he needed to socialize more and had given him a timeline for doing so.

"Just go out to a Denny's for a meal," pretty Dr. Bragg had told him, "or stop in at the local dive and have a beer at the bar."

She shuffled papers on her desk with her perfectly manicured hands, then handed a paper across the desk to him. "That's a set of goals for you and I want you to put it on your refrigerator door and mark the date you accomplish each of them to bring back with you in thirty days for our next session."

"I'm moving to Montana, Doc," Rowdy told her. "Getting back down here to Denver for appointments might be a problem for me."

Her green eyes went wide. "Why Montana?" she asked, and when did you make this decision?"

"It's quiet and there won't be a damned camel in sight." He grinned. "I rented a cabin high up on a mountain in the pines," he said with a sigh, "so I doubt there will be a Denny's to stop in at and I have no idea about dives at this Miller's Crossing."

"Where is that from Missoula? If it's close, I can set you up with an associate of mine at the VA there."

He took out his phone and checked the map feature. "Looks to be about an hour away."

"Good," she said, "I'll call Dr. Cooper and see if he has room for you. If he does, I'll send him your file and text you with an appointment date." She cleared her throat. "But I expect you to use that schedule I gave you and take it in with you to your appointment with Dr. Cooper."

Rowdy stood and saluted with a broad grin on his face. "Yes, ma'am, doctor ma'am."

۞

Now here he stood outside The Devil's Den with his stomach churning after dinner at Millers Crossing's only excuse for an eating establishment, Penny's Gas and Grill. His stomach rumbled and Rowdy had a good idea where the gas came from.

The glass door pushed open and Rowdy had to jump out of the way of two laughing couples as they exited. Give Me Two Steps was just winding down as Rowdy stepped inside the smoky bar. He reconned the room and noticed a redhead in tight jeans at the bar. Taking a deep breath in the foyer, he put one booted foot in front of the other and made his way to the bar, taking the empty stool beside the redhead.

"What can I get ya, young fella?" the gray-headed and bearded bartender asked.

"Bud," Rowdy said, studying the redhead. She had a pretty face with delicate features and a sprinkling of freckles across her sunburned and peeling nose. On her tanned and freckled shoulder, she sported a tattoo he recognized.

"You were with MET?" he asked as the bartender set a frosty mug of beer in front of him. Medical Emergency Transit was a civilian company hired by the military to move the wounded from the battlefields to hospital units. They also supplied medical personnel like EMTs and nurses to tend to the wounded in transit.

"For a while," she said and lifted her left arm onto the bar. It was missing the hand.

"Sorry," he said, suddenly uncomfortable with the situation. "Can I get you another beer?" he asked, noticing the empty mug on the bar in front of her. "Bartender," Rowdy called to the old man, "will you get the lady another of whatever she's having?"

The bartender brought the beer and took the empty mug. "Thank you," she said with a smile, offering her right hand, "I'm Callie."

Rowdy smiled back. It had been a long time since a pretty woman aside from medical staff at the VA had smiled at him. He took her hand. "I'm Rowdy," he said. "Mom was a huge Rawhide fan."

"Seems fittin' for a man in Montana," the old bartender said with a grin. "But you must be new to Miller's Crossin'. Ain't never seen ya in here before."

"I just moved up here from Denver," Rowdy explained.

"Cowboyin' or workin' on one of the pipelines?" the bartender prodded.

"Just kickin' back and takin' it easy for the time being," Rowdy said as he sipped his cold beer. "Might do some hunting and get back into taxidermy."

The old man nodded. "Good money in that with all the hunters and fishermen up here."

"My grandpa taught me," Rowdy said. "I do it for the enjoyment of it in his memory."

"You were in-country then?" Callie finally said, smiling up at him before the bartender could say anymore.

"Gunnery Sergeant with the 107th infantry," he said, puffing his chest out proudly.

Her pretty face lost its smile. "The 107th huh?" She pushed the beer he'd just bought her back to him. "The 107th was supposed to be protecting my convoy when we were attacked," she said with a snarl and raised her left arm into his face. "If you and your men had been there doing your jobs this would never have happened." She slid off the stool and stormed out of the bar as Desperado played on the jukebox.

Rowdy stared after the woman with his mouth open. The only time his unit hadn't made a connection with a MET unit was the day they'd been pinned down by hostiles and he'd lost most of his men. He'd taken a bullet in his upper thigh that day and had almost bled out as well. What right did she have to blame him for the loss of her hand?

"Don't pay no never mind to her, son," the old man said as he took Callie's discarded beer from the bar and put the mug to his lips. "I heard tell she went through some messed up shit at the hands of them camel jockeys over there while they had 'er." He emptied the mug and wiped his mouth with the back of his faded blue sleeve.

"She was a prisoner?" Rowdy asked with his eyes wide. He'd heard terrible stories about what white women had to go through at the hands of Arab captors.

"For nigh on a year as I hear tell," the bartender said, "in the hands of some high up muckity-muck like Bin Laudin, who done terrible things to her and then took off her hand before turnin' her over to her bosses after they paid a big ransom for her safe return."

Rowdy shook his head. "Jeez, no wonder she's bitter."

"I reckon she's got plenty to be bitter about." The old man tapped them both another beer. "I'm Bernie, by the way."

"Nice to meet ya, Bernie," Rowdy said with a salute of his full mug. "So, her name is Callie Miller and she was a POW in Afghanistan?"

Bernie nodded. "And when she finally got sprung, she found out her daddy, ol' man Miller, who owned this whole damned valley and who's family this town, such as it is, was named for, had died in a truck accident and the ranch was bein' run by the foreman Luke Jones." He sucked the foam off the beer. "And ol' Luke was none too happy about turnin' the reins of Miller Ranch over to the young missy after he'd sorta gotten it into his head the place was his for the taken while she was gone an' all."

Rowdy nodded. "Might make for an uncomfortable homecoming." Hadn't the man he'd rented the cabin from been named Luke Jones? Who was his landlord, Luke or Callie? He'd need to take out the lease when he got home and look at it. "What do I owe ya for the beers, Bernie?" Rowdy asked as he stood.

"On the house," the old man said. "Consider it a welcome to the valley gift and a thank you from an ol' Vietnam vet for your service."

"Thanks, man," Rowdy said. "I think I'd have traded some of that jungle shade and humidity any day for that dry, sandy patch of hell I was in."

Bernie chuckled. "No, ya wouldn't. Trench foot from sloggin' around in wet muddy boots all day was nothin' to envy, boy."

"Neither was sand chafe in your crotch or Camel Spiders in your tent at night."

"Eeww, no," Bernie said with a mock shiver. "I hate spiders and I hear them fuckers is as big as a ball mitt."

"Some are," Rowdy said as he turned for the door. "I'll see ya next time, Bernie, and thanks for the beer.

"Don't be takin' your meals down ta Penny's, young fella," Bernie called after him. "That ol' prison cook she has in her kitchen now is like ta kill ya as not."

Rowdy's belly grumbled again. "Now you tell me," he said under his breath as he stepped outside and passed gas.

❧

Callie sat in Penny's, staring at the red stump on the end of her wrist where her hand used to be. How could she have been so unlucky to run into an officer who served with the 107th right here in Miller's Crossing? How was she ever going to get over this when she had reminders of it slapping her in the face or buying her beers every day?

Penny brought her burger and fries to the table. "You look down, hun," the large woman said as she dropped into the chair next to Callie. "What's frettin' you today?"

She lifted her stump. "Same ol', same ol', I suppose, Penn."

"Eat up, Callie," the cafe owner said, "and you'll feel better."

"I met a guy who was with the 107th today," Callie said, rubbing her ruined wrist. "It was him and his men who let this happen. If they'd showed up to give us support the way they were supposed to," she said with tears of anger burning her eyes, "my transport never would have been attacked and I wouldn't have been taken by that damned beast who took my hand."

Penny patted Callie's freckled shoulder. "Maybe if you'd kept the baby, you'd—"

"I'd have the bastard of one of my rapists," Callie snapped. "We've been over this before, Penny. There's no way I could have kept that baby."

"Murdering an innocent was no way to get even with the

man who did that to you, Callie," Penny said with a sigh. "I just hope God can see fit to forgive you."

Callie snorted as she picked up the burger and her purse. "I doubt I'll ever see fit to forgive God," she said. "Put this on my tab, Penny. I'll take it to go." She turned and stormed out of the cafe into the bright Montana sun.

She tossed the cold burger into the trash can outside the cafe and unlocked her Ford Escape four-wheel drive. She was tired of arguing with Penny about her decision to abort the fetus after returning stateside. How could she have expected her to keep that bastard's baby? Callie shook her head. It would have been inconceivable. This was Miller's Crossing, and she was Calista Jane Miller the daughter of Morgan and Rachel Miller.

Callie had been devastated when she returned home to find that her parents had both been killed in an auto accident and in the ground for almost nine months. She'd said her tearful good-byes on her knees in the family burial plot on the ranch where generations of Millers had been laid to rest. She'd needed to talk to her mother so badly and only had a granite headstone to pour her story out to between sobs of grief, anguish, and frustration.

Lucas Jones's attitude upon her return hadn't helped matters any either. "So ya finally decided to show your spoiled ass back up here," he'd snapped from behind Callie as she knelt at her parents' grave. "Your Mama worried after ya like a poor cow what had lost a calf on the trail and your Daddy," he added with hesitation, "well, your Daddy was your Daddy, and he gave them stingy bastards at that MET place you worked a piece of his mind every day you was missin'. Then he raided the ranch bank accounts to give 'em the cash to cover your ransom."

That piece of information had stunned Callie. She'd been under the impression her employers had put up the money for her ransom. "Daddy paid my ransom and not MET?"

Lucas snorted. "You damned well know he did, girl. Drained off near to all the ranch's workin' capital to do it," he sneered, "but Morgan was determined to get his little girl back in one piece." He glanced at her bandaged stump and grinned. "Maybe we should ask for a partial refund since I'm runnin' this place now and we only got back a partial hostage."

Callie had risen to her feet to face the grinning foreman of Miller Ranch. "I'll be taking over now," she said extending her right hand, "so give me the keys to the house and Daddy's office."

Lucas's face had lost its grin and changed to one of anger or even hatred. "I been runnin' this ranch since Morgan and Rachel died, girl, and you got no idea what's involved in keepin' it goin', so why don't ya just stick to your ambulance drivin' in the deserts and let them that knows the business of ranchin' keep at it."

"Mr. Jones," Callie had said with an effort to keep the anger from her voice, "I was raised on this ranch under the wing of Morgan Miller. He taught me everything about running this ranch." Callie had taken a deep breath as she stared down the scowling foreman who'd worked at Miller Ranch for over twenty-five years and whom she'd known most of her life. "I'm very appreciative of what you've done, keeping watch over things after my parents' deaths, but I'm home now and intend to take my place as the owner of Miller Ranch as my father always intended."

Lucas actually laughed. "Ain't no broken little bitch gonna be able to handle the runnin' of this ranch, girl. That's the job of a man like me."

Callie extended her hand again. "The keys, Mr. Jones," she said in a more determined voice, "and please remove your things from the room you took in the house. I'll be taking up residence there now and don't intend to share it with you."

Lucas spat on the ground at her feet as he took the keys

from the ring and tossed them to her. "Things woulda been different had Rachel given him another son like he wanted, but your mama lost every child Morgan got her with except young William after you was born." He shook his head. "I know where you got your stubborn streak, girl. Your Mama was as stubborn as a blue racer and almost as ornery. I'll have my things out of Morgan's house within the hour." He turned to stomp off.

"And leave Daddy's laptop on the kitchen table along with anything else relating to Miller Ranch business you might have in that room like the checkbook and the ATM cards," she called after the man she knew had several pieces of business and ledgers missing from her father's office.

He stopped in his tracks, turned, and gave her a military salute. "Yes, ma'am Miss Miller, ma'am. I'll clear out my things from your daddy's house and leave everything related to your daddy's ranch on your kitchen table."

Callie's grief turned to rage at the insolent foreman, and she called after him, "My house, my ranch, and my kitchen table, Lucas." She thought about firing the bastard on the spot but turned back to the granite stone, went down on her knees again, and wept.

❧ 2 ❧

Tears sprang to Callie's eyes again as she turned onto the gravel road snaking across Miller Ranch and leading to the hundred-year-old ranch house. It had once been a two-family log cabin built with a breezeway connecting the two living spaces, but that had been closed up decades before her mother and father were born, married, and assumed the running of Miller Ranch. Now it was one big home with two floors, four bedrooms, three bathrooms, a huge kitchen, parlor, and office. Aluminum siding and insulated windows had been added in the middle of the Twentieth Century but Callie had often thought it should be taken back closer to its original log design in order to pay tribute to her pioneer relatives who'd braved everything from killer snowstorms in the Montana winters to killer Indians in order to build up one of the largest and successful ranches in the state of Montana. Now she was running Miller ranch and she wondered if she was actually up to it.

Her Escape kicked up dust on the gravel road as she rushed toward home. She slowed the vehicle when she saw something in the road ahead. It was a cow down on her side and when Callie got close enough, she saw blood pooled on the gravel. She stopped the SUV and hopped out when she saw movement at the rear of the injured animal. Callie gasped and went to her knees when she saw a calf trying to free itself from afterbirth.

The cow was dead and had expelled the calf after being struck by a large vehicle. "This is open range," Callie spat as he helped to free the tiny calf from the remains of its mother's womb, "no truck should be moving that fast when stock is present."

She didn't see any other animals and wondered if this was one poor animal that had gotten herself separated from the main herd or if the others had simply scattered after the vehicle had hit this one. Callie sighed with relief when the calf bawled, and she knew it was alive. The mother had been hit hard and Callie worried the calf might have sustained injuries before being born. She rushed to the rear of her vehicle and found an old blanket. She wrapped the calf in it and carried her to the truck, pushing discarded fast-food wrappers and cups aside to make room for the creature bawling for its mother and possibly a first meal. She prayed it wasn't bawling in pain.

"I'm sorry, little one," Callie said as she settled the calf into the back of the Ford, " but I fear you're gonna have to wait until I get you home and Doc Woods can have a look at you before we get you something to eat."

Makenzie, Mak, Woods was the in house vet on Millers Ranch and the son of her family doctor, Brian Woods, in Miller's Crossing. He and Callie had been an item for a minute in High School, but that minute had passed. Mak went off to veterinary school and Callie had gone to Montana State to get a degree in not much of anything, taking classes that interested her but without any real Major. She spoke a spattering of four languages well enough to get by, including Arabic, could recite world history from ancient Babylon to the current Gulf War, and write an intelligent short story or incident report, which had made her uniquely qualified for the job with MET when she'd applied for it.

Her parents had been unhappy about her desire to run off to the underbelly of the world, as her father had put it. She belonged on Miller Ranch, learning the business, and not gallivanting off with a bunch of wounded soldiers in a war zone. Fortunately, her mother had understood Callie's desire to get away from Montana and see a little of the world. Rachel had spent a year after college tramping around Europe with friends and suggested Callie do the same, but Callie had her heart set on helping in Afghanistan with the war effort rather than bumming from town to town through Europe with other spoiled rich kids.

Because of her accumulated college credits, agreeable personality, and ability to step into a leading role in the field when necessary, Callie had moved up quickly at MET and was tasked as a team leader within her first year, silently thanking her father for the lessons she'd learned from him, ordering cowboys around on the ranch. The emerald ring she wore on her finger set her apart from the other women on the team when her convoy had been stopped that day and she'd been taken prisoner for ransom. Her natural red hair, pale complexion, and freckles had made her physically appealing to the bastard, and he'd made her his plaything while waiting for ransom negotiations with MET for her release.

On the day the negotiations had concluded and the money for her release wired, he'd sexually assaulted her repeatedly and then taken her hand. As it turned out, he'd taken her hand and given her a baby on the same day. Callie had returned the baby to God, but there was no way to get her hand back.

She stopped the Escape in front of Mak's office and ran inside. "Are you all right, Callie?" Mak gasped as he jumped to his feet and rushed around his desk. "You're covered in blood. Are you injured?"

Callie glanced down at her shirt and jeans for the first time to see them soaked in red. "It's not mine," she said with a dismissive sweep of her arm. "I found a cow that had been hit on the road and she'd delivered a calf." Callie turned back to the door. "It's alive, but I think she might be injured too."

Makenzie Woods, a tall, thin blond now in his late thirties like Callie, followed her out to the Escape and carried the bawling calf back into his office to examine. "You were right to be concerned, Cal," Mak said after giving the animal a thorough going over with his experienced hands, "it looks like she has a dislocated hip on her rear right side, but that's easy enough to set right." He grinned at Callie. "But you need to get back up to the house and get those clothes into a tub of cold water filled with meat tenderizer or you're gonna have to toss 'em."

"Not a chance," she said, returning his grin, "these are my favorite jeans."

"You say the mother was hit on the road?" Mak asked.

Callie nodded. "About two miles from the ranch up on Pike's Trail," she said, "and it must have been by something pretty big the way she was messed up. "I'm gonna have Lucas send a couple of the boys up there to clean it up before it attracts coyotes, wolves, and buzzards to the ranch."

"I wonder if it was coming from Smalley's ranch," Mak said, "He was in here complaining a few days ago about cattle missing from his range."

"Really?" Callie said. "Rustlers in this day and age?"

Mak shrugged his broad shoulders. "Nothing's changed that much since our grandparents' day." he said, "but now they use helicopters to herd 'em up and semi-trailers to cart 'em off in."

"I'll ask Lucas if he's heard anything about other ranches missing cattle and if Miller Ranch's numbers are in line with what they should be," Callie said with a sigh before turning to leave the vet's office. "Look after our little girl, Mak and I'll be in to check on her later or tomorrow."

"You got it, Callie," Mak called after her. "But hold up a minute, Cal."

Callie turned back to face the vet. "What is it, Mak?"

"I wouldn't press Lucas too hard if I were you," he said with concern etched on his face. "He's still a might raw about having to move back into the bunkhouse."

Callie's mouth fell open. "Was I just supposed to let him keep sleeping in my parents' bed after I got home?"

Mak ran a hand through his wavy blond hair. "Of course not," he said with a sigh, "but he did do a pretty good job of keeping things together after your daddy and mama died while you were gone."

That last bit stung and Callie swallowed hard. "I'll keep that in mind when I talk to him," she said and walked out the door.

Callie got in her car and stopped at the bunkhouse where Lucas now resided. He sat in a chair on the porch with his boots up on the porch railing and curled his lip in a little sneer when Callie got out of her vehicle. "You need my help already, lady ranch owner?" he asked when she neared where he sat.

"Yah," she said with an equal sneer in her tone. "I need my foreman to send some guys up on Pike's trail to clean up a cow that got hit."

"One of our breeders?" he asked.

"Already bred," Callie said. "She threw the calf, but I found it and dropped it off at Doc Woods' to get checked out."

Lucas let out a deep sigh of relief. "It's alive then?"

"Alive and bawling for its mama," Callie said. "I think she'll be fine, but Mak says she has a dislocated hip and he's working on now to fix up."

Lucas grinned. "Then I suppose we got an even trade," he said with a chuckle. "One old breeder for a fresh new one."

He laughed and Callie frowned at his poor taste. "Just have a couple of the guys go up there and clean it up," she said. "We don't need the mess attracting carrion to the property."

"Yes ma'am," Lucas said with a salute he knew would irritate her.

"Mak said some of the local ranchers have been complaining about missing cattle," she said, ignoring the salute. "Has our herd been depleted in any way that you've noticed lately?"

His face lost its grin. "Miller Ranch ain't lost a cow under my watch in twenty-five years, Callie, and it ain't missin' none now neither." He got to his feet. "You know the ranchers like Smalley and Littleton, who can't seem to grow their herds, are always sayin' they've been rustled or attacked by packs of wolves or other such nonsense." As if trying to change the subject he added, "I'll get some of the boys up to Pike Trail to clean up that cow, ma'am, and don't worry any about the Miller herd. We're as sound as we ever were under my supervision." He started to turn away but stopped. "Oh, and I rented that old cabin up on the mountain to a fella that was lookin' for someplace remote and quiet to hold up for a while. You'll find the rental agreement and the record of his payment with the ledgers I left on the table," he said without looking her in the eye and then trudged past her into the bunkhouse and closed the door.

As she pulled away from the bunkhouse, she saw two cowboys leaving and suspected they were the ones Lucas had tasked with moving the carcass.

Inside the empty bunkhouse, Lucas Jones took out his cell phone and punched in a number. "We have a problem, Wheeler," he said when the other party answered. "One of your ass hat drivers hit a cow here on the ranch. I've told you before that you need to have them drive slower around here where we have open range, so they don't draw any unwanted attention."

Lucas listened to Wheeler complain about only being allowed to pick off cattle from the smaller ranches. "I really don't give a shit about your quotas and contracts, Wheeler," he snarled at the man, "the cattle on Miller ranch property are off-limits." He listened some more rolling his eyes and then he grinned. "Don't worry about the spoiled little bitch," he said, "I suspect she'll be having an accident out here on the ranch just like her stupid parents did really soon."

He powered off his phone and shoved it into the back pocket of his jeans. "No little redheaded gimp is gonna take what's rightfully mine away from me now that I've had a taste of what it's like to ride herd on this whole damned thing and see the rewards that are to be had," he said to the empty room before dropping onto his bunk and turning on the television.

Callie changed into clean clothes and put her bloody ones into a tub of cold water and meat tenderizer to soak the bloodstains out. After her laundry chores, she sat down with the ledgers Lucas had left her. It was time she made a serious effort at studying Miller Ranch affairs and reacquainting herself with the business.

Tears stung her eyes when she recognized her father's neat penmanship on the lines of the ledger where he'd recorded the purchases of calves or equipment down the pages as well as the sales of cattle and horses. Morgan Miller had been a meticulous man and paid close attention to the business of Miller Ranch. As she turned the pages she saw the change in the handwriting. The dates corresponded with the death of her parents.

After an hour of studying the books and comparing numbers, Callie came to suspect Lucas had been skimming money from the sales of cattle. If that were indeed the case, Lucas Jones would soon find himself out of a job and off

Miller Ranch for good. He'd been employed by Miller Ranch for over twenty-five years and it was probably time for him to retire and be put out to pasture anyhow. Callie was certainly tired of his smart mouth. Tomorrow she would begin talking with different cowboys on the ranch to get an idea about who might make a good replacement foreman and if none of them seemed up to snuff she'd put ads in some of the local papers and trade journals.

Callie turned a page and found a folded piece of paper. She opened it and read through it to find it the lease agreement on the cabin Lucas had rented. Her eyes went wide when she saw the name of the renter—Rowdy Waters. Hadn't that been the name of the man in the bar? She stared at her wrist and wanted to tear up the lease and throw it in the trash. She closed her eyes and saw the face of the handsome man from the bar again. Maybe she should just get in her car, drive up to the cabin and tell him Lucas had been mistaken and the family hunting cabin hadn't been for rent after all. He'd seemed like a reasonable man.

3

After leaving the bar, Rowdy got in his old Jeep Cherokee and headed toward the cabin. His mind was still a swirl with the freckled redhead he met in the Devil's Den. Callie Miller was a woman full of the Devil if he'd ever seen one. Recent rains had left the steep, narrow road up to the mountain cabin muddy and Rowdy drove slower than normal for safety's sake. Lucas had warned him to stock up on groceries before the winter because the snows they got up here could leave the road impassable for weeks or even months at a time.

Part of his rental agreement was to do much-needed maintenance to the old cabin, stable, and corals for a manageable rent of only five hundred dollars a month. His VA disability wasn't very much every month, but five hundred left him plenty for groceries, gasoline, and trips into Home Depot for supplies.

Rowdy enjoyed working with his hands and the old property gave him plenty of things to work on. There'd been no running water in the cabin, but there was a nearby creek fed by snow runoff. It hadn't taken him more than a day and fifty dollars in plastic pipe to rig up a ram pump and now he had running water in the cabin. Trekking to an outhouse in the snow hadn't been very appealing to Rowdy, so he'd built a simple composting toilet and dug a compost pit in the back which would eventually break down into good garden soil if he kept adding vegetation and kitchen waste to the mix.

Electricity for power tools had been an issue but he'd found an old Honda generator in the stable and after a few hours of tinkering and several cans of oil, he had it purring like a kitten. A couple of solar panels along with batteries and a simple charge controller were on his list of items to purchase with his next check. With those, he might be able to enjoy some television and his stereo.

Growing up on a farm in rural southeast Missouri had been boring but it had taught him a lot about being self-sufficient. Rowdy parked his Jeep beside the cabin, got out, and said hello to his newest addition—a dozen chickens in the coop he'd constructed from old lumber he'd scavenged from around the property and chicken wire from a salvage lot he'd found on the edge of Miller's Crossing. Every town had one filled with the unwanted junk of everyone living in the area and Rowdy intended to make use of this one as much as he could. A chipped enameled sink now graced his countertop in the kitchen area, and he had a forty-gallon hot water heater in pieces on the floor inside. When repaired Rowdy would hook it up to propane bottles and have hot running water in the kitchen sink and the shower he planned to build in the corner of the bedroom.

The cabin still had a musty smell from being closed up for God only knew how long. Lucas had told him it was the Miller family's hunting cabin but since the death of Morgan Miller and his wife it hadn't been used. He told Rowdy that he'd wanted to rent it to keep poachers and horny teenagers out of it.

As he stepped inside, his cell phone rang, and Rowdy pulled it from his pocket. He didn't recognize the number, but only a few of his friends, his doctors at the VA, and his aged mom had his number. If one of them needed him he'd better answer.

"Hello," he said as he lit an oil lamp in the counter and pushed aside the curtains for some light.

"Rowdy?" said a hesitant male voice. "Rowdy this is Billy —Billy Dane from the unit. How are ya, man?"

"Billy?" Rowdy said, trying to put a face to the name. Oh, yah, Billy Dane had been a grunt in their unit who'd taken a hit in the shoulder during the firefight. Hadn't he almost lost the arm after those VA butchers had gotten ahold of him? "Oh, hey Billy. What's up?"

"Well, I heard you were in the Missoula area and wondered if you might need some work."

Rowdy stared around at the pieces of water heater scattered over the floor. "What kind of work?" he asked. "And who told you I was near Missoula?"

"Doc Bragg from the VA told me," he said with a juvenile chuckle. "She gave me your number too. You ever tap that, bud, because I think she was hot for your ass."

Rowdy rolled his eyes, remembering the kid's fixation with sex now. Where did he get the idea that Dr. Bragg had the hots for him? Rowdy had certainly never gotten that impression from the pretty, uptight doctor. It pissed him off some that the doctor would be handing out his private number, but Rowdy supposed she was trying to help by hooking him up with another vet with a job to offer.

"So, tell me about this job, Billy and I'm actually about an hour out of Missoula. If the job is there I don't think it would be feasible for me to take it."

"Awe no, it's actually out in ranch country workin' with cattle, herding them up and moving them into trucks for transport into the stockyards for slaughter."

"I'm no cowboy, Billy," Rowdy said, staring at the scattered parts on the floor, "and I sorta have my hands full with the place I'm living. I trade out rent for carpenter work on the place."

"Wow, man, that sounds cool." He gave a little chuckle. "Sure sounds better than shoveling cow shit out of the transport trailers like they've had me doing of late. My boss told me that if I could bring in a new recruit, then he'd step me up to something else."

"And you thought of me?" Rowdy said, rolling his eyes again as he picked up the rusted out bottom of the water heater. "Thanks, Bill, but I think I have my hands full here for the time being."

"OK man," Billy said, sounding somewhat despondent, "but if you change your mind, you have my number in your phone now. You can give me a call anytime and I can get you on here. The money ain't bad and they're pretty easy to work for."

"I'll keep that in mind," Rowdy said as he disconnected.

He spent the remainder of his afternoon and most of the next day cutting and soldering tin to patch the old heater. When he finally had it watertight, he hooked it up to a propane tank and prayed there were no problems with the valves or fittings. Rowdy let out a cheer when the gas caught and by the time he needed to wash dishes, warm water trickled from the faucet into the sink.

By the time he stripped down for a sponge bath, the water was hot and Rowdy thought he deserved a treat. He washed his growing brown curls and decided to look up a barber the next time he was in Miller's Crossing on business. He hadn't cut his hair since leaving the service and couldn't say he missed the military buzz cut, but the bush on his head now was in need of a trim. Before joining the service he'd always worn his hair longer than most with the curls brushing his shoulders. His mom had always liked long hair on men and had never complained about the length the way the mothers of some of his friends did.

Sherry Waters had been a great mom, giving him plenty of rope but not enough to hang himself with. She'd been a single mother in the Bible belt and taken plenty of flak from the pent up, repressed women around her. Most shunned her and treater her like trash, but Sherry Waters had done her own thing and bought the rundown farmhouse and ten acres with some help from her grandfather. She raised Rowdy there and taught him about growing things and raising animals for food. She taught him how to shoot a gun and how to hunt rabbits, squirrel, and quail for their freezer.

Sherry's grandfather, a taxidermist, had taught Rowdy to mount his kills and had been the male influence in Rowdy's life since his biological father had never been in the picture while he was growing up. Rowdy had met that man once in a local bar and punched him out when he'd made a crude comment about Sherry to the other men there.

Rowdy had no use for the man. He'd left Sherry to fend for herself with a new infant and Rowdy thought she'd done a damned fine job of it without the bastard's help. Over sixty now, Sherry still tended her garden and chickens, selling produce and eggs at the local farmers' market along with craft items she made in her little studio at home.

Rowdy had always sent her money every month to help out and when her grandfather had passed away a few years ago, he'd left her a little nest egg. As Rowdy dressed in clean clothes for a trip down to the Devil's Den for a well-deserved beer, he made a mental note to call his mom tomorrow.

When he reached the bar, he had to park in the street because the small gravel lot was full. Rowdy had never ventured down the mountain and into town at night before and he smiled to himself, checking another thing off Dr. Bragg's list.

Music blared inside from a band playing country music on the small stage in the back corner of the building decorated with rodeo posters and neon beer signs. The cigarette smoke was thick and stung Rowdy's eyes.

"Don't you have an exhaust fan in this joint, Bernie?" Rowdy asked the bartender when he took a seat at the polished bar constructed from an old slice of pinewood coated in epoxy resin.

The old man turned at the mention of his name and smiled. "Busted on me nigh on two years back," he said, "and ain't got no one hereabouts who'll work on it fer me." Bernie tapped a Bud into a mug and slid it across the bar.

Rowdy took a long swallow of the beer and smiled. "I'm pretty good with stuff like that," he said, "and I'm rather fond of breathing clean, so how about I come take a look at it for ya sometime soon?"

"Couldn't pay ya much," the old man said, "the overhead here in this place is killin' me."

What overhead? He saw one skinny waitress in tight jeans trying to dodge the hands of cowboys on her ass and the band likely played for tips and a few drinks. The lights were dimmed and from the temp of the beer in his mug, Rowdy suspected the old man kept his cooler set as high as possible to save on the electric bill.

At the end of the song, the band leader said they were taking a quick break and the quiet in the room was deafening.

"Uh oh," Bernie said, "here comes trouble fer sure."

Rowdy turned to see Callie Miller walk in the door. She wore tight jeans and a flannel shirt open to reveal a skin-tight tank top beneath. Her wavy red hair was combed and flowed like a rust-tinted waterfall over her shoulders. Damn, she was a hot piece. Rowdy stared as she walked toward the bar and felt his cock begin to stiffen as she came closer. She stopped and frowned when she saw him, her eyes darting around the crowded bar for an empty seat anyplace but close to him.

A tall man in his fifties separated from the cowboys he stood with. He planted himself directly in Callie's path with his hands on his hips. "Well, if it ain't the high and mighty lady ranch owner come into town to grace us lowlife cowboys with her glowing presence," he said with a loud sneer.

"I tolt ya there was gonna be trouble," Bernie said, taking a sawed-off shotgun from beneath the bar. "Lucas Jones has been in here mouthin' off about Callie Miller and how she stolt his birthright from him for the past two hours."

Rowdy screwed his face up in confusion. "How does he figure she stole his birthright?"

"It's a long story havin' to do with Callie's grandpa who dipped his wick in every wet hole in the county and Lucas's mama who happened to have one of them wet holes."

"Oh," Rowdy said, suddenly feeling uncomfortable with the conversation.

"Why don't you go sit down, Lucas," Callie said as equally loud and voices hushed across the room in anticipation of what was to come.

"You're trying' to steal what's rightfully mine, little girl," Lucas said, pointing at Callie, "and I'm takin' it to a lawyer tomorrow, so you can just forget about stealin' what's mine."

Callie slapped his hand from her face. "I don't know what the hell you're talking about, Lucas, but if anyone's the thief around here it's you. I went through the books you left and there are several discrepancies." It was Callie's turn to point a finger. "You're a thief, Lucas, Jones and you're fired. Don't bother coming back on my property. "I'll have one of the boys pack up your things and bring them here for you to pick up." She yelled into his face. "I don't ever want to see you on my ranch again. Do you hear me?"

Lucas tossed the beer from his mug into Callie's face. "Just cool down a little, bitch," he said, laughing at the beer running down Callie's face and onto her heaving breasts. "This excitement can't be good for someone as delicate as the sweet and pampered Calista Miller."

"Fuck you, asshole," Callie spat back. "You're a lying thief and nobody wants you on Miller Ranch. My parents never wanted you there and I don't want you there. You're a leech and you're fired."

Lucas balled up his fist, drew back, and punched Callie in the face, sending the redhead to the floor as gasps from the bar were heard. "I heard you, bitch, but that damned ranch is mine and I intend to have it." He kicked the woman hard. "Ain't no crippled cunt who can't even ride a horse no more or keep track of her cows gonna take it from me."

Before he could land another kick, Rowdy grabbed his shoulder and pulled him away. "It's not gentlemanly to beat on a woman, Mister."

Lucas shook Rowdy's hand off. "I seriously doubt this is even a woman," he said with a drunken snort as he turned to his friends. "How bout we yank down them jeans and see if there's a cunt in 'em or a little dick."

His friends laughed and moved closer to the unconscious woman. "How 'bout all you assholes just leave the lady be and take your sorry selves outa my bar," Bernie said, racking the shotgun and pointing it at the back of Lucas' head.

Lucas Jones and the other cowboys left the bar, grumbling as the band started playing again. "Can you see the lady home or to Doc Woods' clinic, young man?" Bernie said softly to Rowdy.

Rowdy scooped Callie up into his arms. "I'll take care of her, Sir," he said respectfully to the old man.

Bernie nodded and returned to the bar as Rowdy carried Callie out and put her into his Jeep, securing her in the seat-belt. What was he supposed to do with her now? He wasn't even certain how to get to her ranch house from here.

Rowdy got behind the wheel and started the engine. "Well, I guess you're coming home with me tonight, Sleeping Beauty."

❧ 4 ❧

Callie woke to the sound of snoring and batted her eyes open in the dim room. Her head throbbed and she sat up in the unfamiliar bed to see Rowdy Waters asleep in a rocking chair beside the bed. He was certainly a handsome man, well built with a head of thick brown curls. Callie grunted with pain in her midsection and it roused the sleeping man.

"Are you all right?" he asked as he straightened himself in the old rocker made from bent grapevines.

That is my grandma's rocker," she said as she pulled the blanket up over her bare breasts, getting angrier by the minute. "Why are you sleeping in it and where are my damned clothes?"

"They were wet with the beer Lucas threw on you," he explained, "so I put them in the washer and laid them out in front of the fireplace to dry." He stood and stretched. "I don't have electricity here yet to run the dryer." He scratched his head. "As for the rocker, I found it out in the barn, fixed the broken rocker, and rewove the seat so you don't fall through."

"Wow," she said with a sigh. "I thought grandpa chopped it up and burned it in the fireplace decades ago." She grinned.

"My Grandma loved that old chair, but my Grandpa hated it and was always threatening to burn it in a bonfire and roast marshmallows over it."

"Maybe he loved her enough to hang on to it in the hopes of getting it fixed for her someday."

She snorted. "You wouldn't say that if you'd heard some of the fights I did."

Callie stared around the bedroom of the family hunting cabin in the dim morning light coming through the window. "You have a washer and dryer up here?" She scratched her aching head. "Wait a minute," she said in confusion, "where'd you get running water for a damned washing machine?"

Rowdy grinned. "I've been making a few improvements," he said. "I'll go to the other room and get your clothes. The toilet is over there by the wardrobe if you need it"

"Toilet?" she gasped and craned her head to see the simple wooden construction with a toilet seat. Wow, he had been making improvements.

"Composting," he said as he left the room and closed the door.

"So, in other words," she called as she padded to the toilet, "I'm pissing in a damned bucket."

"Yes," he called back, laughing, "but with a very comfortable seat from Home Depot on top."

As she released her morning water, Callie had to admit this was quite comfortable and much better than having the traipse through the wet grass and weeds to the outhouse, always on the alert for snakes in her path.

"Here," he said, handing her clothes in with the door closed enough for modesty's sake. "They're dry and don't smell like a brewery anymore."

"Thanks," Callie said, taking the clothes from his outstretched hand. "I really do appreciate it."

When Callie tried to put on her jeans, she saw a huge purple bruise just above her left hip. What the hell had happened to her? The last thing she recalled was her altercation with Lucas, but it was fuzzy. He'd called her a thief. Why? She'd never stolen anything from him. She slipped on her tank top and then the warm flannel shirt against the slight chill in the mountain air.

The crowing of a rooster startled her. Did he have chickens up here? Callie didn't know how she felt about this strange man making himself at home in her family's cabin. Chickens? A toilet? A washing machine. What else had he done to change the place she'd loved to come as a child and escape life on the ranch below?

Callie stepped out of the bedroom into a room she hardly recognized. The old wood cookstove remained but every window had been washed and red gingham curtains hung. Curtains in the hunting cabin? Her grandfather would have been scandalized. The floors had been sanded, stained, and varnished to a glossy finish.

"Coffee?" he asked as he filled a pot from a faucet at a sink she'd never seen in the cabin before.

Her mouth dropped open in amazement. "How in the name of heaven did you get running water up here?" she asked. "I always had to bring it in buckets up from the creek."

He smiled as he carried the coffee pot to the stove, put in the basket of ground coffee, and left it to perk. "It's still coming from the creek," he said, "but I made a ram pump and buried some pipe. Come here," he said, motioning for her to come to the sink as he turned on the faucet.

Callie walked hesitantly to the sink and put her hand into the stream of water. Her eyes went wide. "It's hot," she exclaimed, pulling her hand back. "You put in a hot water heater?"

"Well, I rebuilt one I found at that salvage yard and set it up outside," he said with a nod to the outside wall.

"Do you run the old Honda for electricity to run the washer?" she asked, staring at the stacked unit set up at the end of the cabinets that made up the kitchen space in the cabin.

"I run it in my shop out in the barn for my power tools," he said. "I plan to set up a small solar array and get some batteries for electricity here in the cabin." Rowdy grinned and Callie noted a set of bright white teeth in his mouth. He had a nice smile and for the first time in a long time, she found herself wondering what it would feel like to kiss a man.

The rooster crowed again and broke Callie's chain of thought. "You have chickens?" she asked, trying to gather her scattered thoughts.

He picked up an egg from a basket on the counter. "I like mine scrambled," he said with a grin. "How do you take yours? My girls have been very productive of late."

"Scrambled is fine with me," she said as she took her old place at the round table he'd dressed with a tablecloth of red and white gingham to match the curtains. My grandpa is probably turning over in his grave," Callie said with a smile. "He'd never let my grandma put curtains up in here. He said it was a man's hunting cabin and no place for frillies like curtains and such."

Rowdy laughed. " My mama would have slapped his mouth and told him a window was like a woman and should be dressed pretty for everyone to look at."

Callie smiled. "My grandma would have liked your mama then." She sipped the steaming cup of coffee he put in front of her. "Do you have any milk? This is a little strong."

He opened the door of the propane refrigerator and took out a carton of milk. "I hauled that old icebox out to the barn," he said, "and covered it up good. If I know my antiques, I'd say that thing would fetch a good price from a collector."

Callie nodded. "This cabin was built sometime in the late eighteen hundreds and I think that icebox has been here since before the turn of the century." She ran a hand through her knotted red hair. "They used this cabin as a lookout post for Indians and cattle rustlers," she said with a sigh.

Rowdy laid out strips of bacon in the cast-iron skillet. "It must be nice," he muttered.

"What must be nice?" she asked with a furrow in her brow, sensing irritation in his comment.

"To have family you can go back generations and tell folks about." Rowdy stabbed at the sizzling bacon.

"The Millers settled in Montana sometime after the Civil War," she said. "I think they got burned out or run out of Missouri and somehow ended up here."

He turned away from the stove and smiled. "I'm from Missouri."

"And your mama who believes in dressing up windows? Is she still there in Missouri?"

Rowdy nodded. "Near a little town called Jackson," he said with a far off look in his eyes. "I should have gone back there after I was discharged from the VA to help her out on the farm, but I just couldn't bring myself to return there after finally getting away."

"Your father's not there to help her out?" Callie asked, but knew immediately from the dark look on Rowdy's handsome face that she shouldn't have.

"That son-of-a-bitch walked out on her as soon as she told him she was pregnant with me," Rowdy said with a growl. "I don't even know if he's still breathing."

"I'm sorry I opened an old wound," Callie said. "Please don't burn the bacon on my account."

Rowdy whipped back around to tend to his skillet and moved the smoking pan off the stove. "It's a little brown and crisp," he muttered, "but not really burned."

Callie smiled. "I like my bacon brown and crisp."

Rowdy cracked eggs into a heavy crock bowl Callie had seen her grandmother use hundreds of times. He added milk and a handful of crated cheddar cheese before pouring the mixture into the hot skillet and stirring it with a fork.

"I hope these are to your liking, Miss Miller," he said with a smile as he set a plate of scrambled eggs and crisp bacon in front of her.

Callie smiled back. "It looks and smells fantastic," she said as she picked up a slice of bacon and bit into it. "Just the way I like it," she said with a wink of her emerald-green eyes.

Rowdy sat down and dug into his plate of food like a starving man. "So how did a woman like you with a big ranch in Montana and deep family roots end up in Afghanistan with MET?"

Callie stared down at her wrist for the first time that morning and found herself shocked that she hadn't thought about it or the circumstances around it at all. How could she not, when this man had been one of the group responsible? If the 107th had shown up when they were supposed to and escorted her convoy of wounded, she'd never have been taken prisoner by Al-Asadi, beaten, raped repeatedly, ransomed, and then had her hand taken by the bastard.

Callie cleared her throat. "I'd been out of college for a few years and living on the ranch with Mom and Dad," she said. "Mak and I had been dating off and on since high school and when he got back after vet school, we flirted around with getting married." She took a deep breath. "It was something both our parents wanted, but not either of us."

"Mak the vet on your ranch?" Rowdy asked with a furrowed brow. "That sounds like it would have been a good fit."

Callie snorted. "Mak would likely be more interested in jumping your bones than mine," she said with a grin.

"Oh, I see," Rowdy said with his cheeks turning red.

"Doc Woods thought I could screw the gay out of Mak," Callie said, "and my dad just wanted a male heir to leave Miller Ranch to—if not my son, then my husband." She emptied her coffee cup. "Maybe he should have just left the ranch to Lucas if he's really my grandfather's illegitimate son."

"You never knew Lucas Jones was your uncle?" Rowdy asked.

Callie shook her head. "Even families with deep roots have secrets in their closets, Mr. Waters."

"He sounds pretty bitter about the whole thing," Rowdy said. "Why do you think he hates you so much?"

Callie shrugged her shoulders. "Maybe because I was born on the right side of the sheets and got to carry the Miller name instead of him. I don't know."

"Maybe it's just because you're female and put in a position of power over him." Rowdy shook his head. "I saw that a lot in the military. Guys would hate a commanding officer for no other reason than that officer was female and had power over them."

Callie got up and refilled her cup. "I don't know, but I think I should go back into town and swear out a warrant against him for these bruises." She carried the pot to the table and refilled Rowdy's cup as well. "I swore when I finally got away from that bastard Al-Asadi, that no man would ever bruise me again and get away with it."

Rowdy frowned. "That's a name I never thought I'd hear again," he said. "Al-Asadi was the man who set up the attack on my troopers and pinned us down that day." He shook his head. "I just wish I'd been there to see that bastard get his ass blown to hell in that drone strike. The son-of-a-bitch was responsible for taking the lives of some really good men in my unit and nearly took mine." Rowdy rubbed his thigh where the bullet entered and shattered the bone, leaving him with a limp he'd have for the rest of his life and a monthly disability check. "I hope his seventy-two virgins were all dried up old spinster schoolteachers with ruler in their hands to smack him every time he said a dirty word."

Callie giggled. "That would have been a lot of smacking then," she said. "He liked to talk dirty while he was having sex with me. He was especially fond of calling me his ruby cunt."

"I'm so sorry that happened to you, Miss Miller," Rowdy said, looking away. "It must have been horrible for you."

"You rescued me from a beating last night," she said with a smile, "and I spent the night in your bed. I think you can call me Callie now."

"Thank you, Callie, but it's nothing any real man wouldn't have done." He emptied his coffee cup and set it aside. "My mama taught me to go to the aid of any woman in need. It's what real men do."

Callie snorted. "And just how many real men were there beside you in the Devil's Den last night, Mr. Waters?"

Rowdy grinned uneasily. "Only old Bernie with his sawed-off shotgun and it's Rowdy not Mr. Waters. That was my grandpa and he'd have knocked Lucas Jones's teeth down his throat for what he did to you. Thomas Waters was a real man if there ever was one."

"He sounds like he was a good teacher," Callie said with a smile. "Old Bernie is sure a gem of a man."

Rowdy smiled. "He reminds me of my grandpa."

Callie pushed her chair back and stood. "Thank you for everything," she said, "and I hate to leave you with this mess to clean up, but I'd better get back to the ranch to make certain the boys have cleared Lucas's things out and he's off Miller Ranch."

"Do you think that's safe, Callie? Why don't you hold up here for a few days until he's cooled off some?"

"I'm no coward, Rowdy," she said with fire in her green eyes, "and I'm not going to hide out from the likes of Lucas Jones." She carried her dirty dishes to the sink. "Now if you'd be so kind as to drive me back to the Den so I can get my car, I'd appreciate it."

"Have all the Miller women down through history been as

stubborn and pig-headed as you?" Rowdy collected his dirty dishes and carried them to the sink to join Callie's.

Callie smiled. "If you mean that they were unwilling to take anyone's crap or back down from a fight, then yes they were." She ran her fingers through her red curls to straighten them into order. "My great-great-grandmother Margaret Miller, bore ten children, traveled from Missouri to Montana with most of them crowded into a covered wagon, braved frigid Montana winters in a drafty log cabin, held off wild Indians who wanted to chase them off this land, and lived with an even wilder husband from what I'm told to build Miller Ranch from nothing." She picked up her purse and flung the strap over her shoulder. "Now, if you'd drive me down the mountain, I have a damned ranch to run."

Rowdy smiled. Calista Miller reminded him of his mama. She was strong and independent. He walked over, took her into his arms and kissed her on the mouth. She didn't resist and even returned the kiss, opening her mouth and allowing his tongue inside to play with hers. When his cock began to stiffen in his jeans, Rowdy pulled back, smiled down into those beautiful emerald eyes and said, "Well, you did sleep in my bed last night."

Callie grinned back. "I suppose you deserved a kiss after saving my ass from Lucas last night."

He blew out the oil lamp on the counter and adjusted the damper on the stove before opening the door for Callie. "So tell me, Miss Miller," he asked with an impish grin, "are you gonna give ole Bernie a kiss like that for backing me up last night with that sawed-off shotgun of his?"

5

Rowdy enjoyed the drive down the mountain with Callie in the seat beside him. His mind returned to the kiss they'd shared, and he hoped there would be more of those in the future. Rowdy stopped his Jeep beside a blue Ford Escape, the only vehicle parked in the gravel lot outside The Devil's Den. "I really wish you'd reconsider going back to the ranch until you've gone to the sheriff about what happened here last night with Lucas, Callie."

Callie took out her cell phone. "I'll call the sheriff's office on my way home and file a report," she said.

"I thought you said you were going to go down there and make a report in person," he said, frowning.

"Everyone knows me down there," Callie said, "and I'm sure all of them have already heard all about what happened here last night." She giggled as she opened the door. "Word about shit like that travels fast here in Miller's Crossing."

Rowdy reached across the seat and took her left arm above where her hand once was. "I'd really feel better if you'd go to the office and make the report in person, Callie. I'll even go with you if you want."

"Don't be ridiculous," she said, pushing the door open and jerking her arm from his grasp. "I'll call down there and if they need you to come in I'll give you a call." She handed him her phone. "Put your number in there for me."

Rowdy punched in his number and added his name to her contact list, hoping she'd call for more than the visit to the sheriff's office, and handed the phone back to her.

"Thanks," Callie said. She got out of the Jeep and Rowdy followed her to the Escape. Maybe he'd get another kiss.

"Callie, I really wish you'd reconsider going back to the ranch. I think you should lay low for a few days until Lucas settles down some."

Callie unlocked the door and slid into the vehicle. "I have a ranch to run, Mr. Waters," she snarled. "I can't run off up to the mountain and hide out with my tail tucked between my legs just because Lucas Jones made some drunken threats in a bar." She started the Escape, jammed it into gear, and threw gravel as she spun her tires on her way out of the parking lot.

After watching her go, he glanced at his feet and noticed an oily stain on the gravel beneath where Callie's truck had been parked. Rowdy knelt, touched the gravel and put it to his nose. "Shit," he said to himself and the empty parking lot, "brake fluid for sure. That son-of-a-bitch Lucas or one of his crew cut her damned brake line." He jogged back to his Jeep and jumped in, racing out of the parking lot after Callie.

Callie rushed toward the ranch, thinking back to the kiss. She hadn't thought she'd ever want to be kissed by a man again, but Rowdy Waters had excited her like no man had in a very long time. He was kind, considerate, handsome, and he had chickens and gingham curtains. Who couldn't be attracted to a man with chickens in his back yard and pretty curtains on his windows? She smiled to herself. The kiss hadn't been bad either.

She turned onto Pike Trail and looked forward to getting

home and taking a hot shower. Her body ached all over. Maybe she'd run a tub filled with hot water and just soak for an hour. Ahead of her Callie saw a huge cloud of dust pluming up from behind a large truck. Why was the idiot driving so fast on a ranch road? Was he the one who'd hit the pregnant cow? As the truck drew nearer, Callie laid down on her horn, hoping it would alert the driver to reduce his speed. Rather than slowing down, the driver moved over into Callie's path in a ridiculous game of chicken on the narrow graveled road.

Callie pressed on the brake as she moved to the edge of the trail, but the pedal went flat to the floor and her Escape didn't slow. At her rate of speed, she panicked and over-corrected. She screamed when she felt the Escape tip up and begin to roll across the grass. The truck sounded its horn as it flew by throwing dust across her windshield as she rolled. Her head jerked around as the airbag exploded in her face and Callie lost consciousness.

She woke with her face throbbing and blood dripping onto the deflating airbag. It took Callie a few minutes to sort out her situation. She hung upside down, suspended in place by the seatbelt.

Callie clawed at the seatbelt release with her good hand but the stress of her weight on the belt kept the latch from releasing. She struggled and tried to pull the release again without success.

"Damnit," Callie screamed in frustration. "What am I supposed to do now?" She glanced down and saw water trickling in from around the bent doorframes. "Now this is just great." Why hadn't she just gone back up to the cabin with Rowdy when he asked her? She could be enjoying his company and maybe even another good meal.

Tears filled her eyes when Callie glanced through the side window to see the granite monument piled with flowers the ranch hands had erected in the spot where her parents had wrecked their car on the way home from a cattle auction and been killed. She suddenly remembered Lucas's words in The Devil's Den about being the next Miller to die and how she'd be joining them in the family plot soon. Could he have arranged for that truck to wait for her and run her off the road? How could he have managed that? He couldn't have known when she'd be picking up her car or when she'd be on Pike's Trail.

Callie struggled in the seatbelt and she swung back and forth causing her already aching body to throb. Her vision blurred and her head hurt worse than she could ever remember hurting before. She must have hit it while the Escape rolled along with the airbag exploding in her face and wrenching her neck. She was really going to need that soak in a hot tub now but groaned when she noted the water rising below her. "Instead, I'm probably going to drown in a cold damned drainage ditch," she said with tears of frustration dripping down to join the water.

Callie's eyes blurred as the blood collected in her head. She barely registered the pounding on the windshield and went unconscious as it exploded inward with Rowdy's heavy boot kick. He made his way through the shattered windshield, felt for a pulse, and tried to revive Callie by patting her cheeks, but she was out cold. He released the belt and eased her body down into the water filling the Escape, hoping the chilled water would bring her around. It didn't and he took a deep breath before pulling her out into the creek and dragging her to the surface, hoping he wasn't aggravating any injuries she might have sustained in the accident.

Rowdy lifted her carefully from the ditch and carried her to his Jeep. "This seems to be becoming old hat with us," Rowdy said as he eased Callie into the passenger seat and secured her in with the seatbelt. Her red hair hung over her shoulders, dripping, and Rowdy brushed water from her bruised and bleeding face. Even with the bruises, Callie Miller was an incredibly beautiful woman. She coughed up water and Rowdy moved her forward to keep her from choking. "Get it all out, Sweetie," Rowdy said as he patted her back.

Callie lifted her head and her eyes fluttered open. She began to struggle in the seatbelt, clawing at the latch. "Get me the hell out of here," she gasped and coughed.

"You're out, Callie," Rowdy told her in a calming voice as he held both her shoulders. "You're out of your car and in mine, Sweetie."

She jerked her head up and batted her eyes in the sun. "I'm out?" she mumbled. "How?"

"I'm afraid I had to kick in your windshield," he said with a soft chuckle, "but I think that's the least of your worries with that poor truck. I think it's pretty much trashed."

"The truck," she groaned. "Did you see the truck that tried to hit me? The Escape wouldn't stop," she mumbled. Her head began to sag. "Lucas said I was going to join my parents." She pointed to a granite marker beside the road. "They died there," she mumbled, "and I almost died there too." She wrapped her arms around Rowdy's neck and wept as she shivered in her wet clothes. "I thought I was going to die in the cold water."

Rowdy kissed the top of her wet head. "Nobody is going to die today, Callie," he whispered, "but we need to get you to a doctor and out of those wet clothes. Did you say there was a doctor on your ranch?"

"Mak," she mumbled. "Mak has a clinic at the entrance of the ranch."

Rowdy loosed her arms from around his neck and settled her back into the seat. "Then let's get you to the doctor," he said and rushed around to get behind the wheel. He drove to the ranch entry and saw what looked like an old stable structure. The sign mounted above the porch read Woods Clinic.

He pulled into the gravel lot, got out, and scooped Callie up into his arms to carry her into the clinic.

The lobby was empty except for a blonde man sitting behind the counter with a copy of Golf Digest in his hand. "You the doctor?" Rowdy asked in a demanding voice. "I got a hurt woman here."

The man stood and rushed around the counter. "What happened?"

"Rolled her truck out there on the road," Rowdy said. "I think she has a head injury."

"Bring her back here," the man said and led Rowdy down a hall and into a small room with a twin bed. "This may be an animal hospital," the blond said, "but here on the ranch I have human patients from time to time with broken bones, cuts, and scrapes."

Rowdy stopped and stared at the tall man in his white coat. "You're a vet?" he gasped. "Callie needs a real doctor," he said, holding the woman closer. "Where do I find one of those around here?"

The vet came close to stare down at Callie's face. "Callie Miller?" he gasped. "Put her on the bed and I'll call my dad." He pulled out a cell phone and punched in numbers. "I'm Dr. Woods the vet," he said, "but my dad is Dr. Woods the medical doctor in Miller's Crossing and he's Callie's family doctor." He pointed to the bed as he held the phone to his ear. "Put her down there. We need to get her out of those wet clothes." He became more alert and adjusted the phone. "Dad, I need you out here at the ranch," he said staring down at the woman on the bed. "Callie's been in an accident and it looks like a head injury." He smiled at Rowdy and nodded. "Thanks, Dad. Yah, I can do film here."

The doctor offered his hand. "I'm Doctor Makenzie Woods," he said, "but everyone around here calls me Mak."

"Rowdy Waters," he said, taking the man's hand. "I'm renting her cabin up on the mountain."

"Nice to meet you Rowdy," Mak said as he stared down at Callie. "What the hell happened to her face?" he demanded as he took alcohol and pads from a cabinet. "That doesn't look like just an airbag injury."

Rowdy took a deep breath. "She had a run-in with Lucas Jones at The Devil's Den last night and he punched her in the face after she fired him."

Mak shook his head. "I told her to watch out for that son-of-a-bitch."

"She has a big bruise on her lower abdomen just above her hip where he kicked her too," Rowdy told him.

"Help me get her out of these wet clothes, Rowdy, so I can have a look at it." They peeled off Callie's wet clothes without her coming to and Mak studied the purple bruise in the shape of a size eleven boot print. "Damn," Mak hissed, "he kicked her good, huh?"

"I think he'd have killed her if Bernie and me hadn't pulled him off her," Rowdy said, "and I think he cut the brake line on her truck."

"What?" Mak gasped as he covered Callie with a blanket. "Tell me about it when I get back with the X-ray Machine, so I can get pictures of her head and that kick before my dad gets here."

Mak left the room and Rowdy pulled a chair close to the bed. He took one of the alcohol pads and gently wiped the blood from Callie's swollen face. Her eyes fluttered open and her green eyes darted around the sparse room. "Where am I?" she whispered.

"The vet's clinic," Rowdy told her. "Would you rather I drove you into Miller's Crossing to the medical clinic so you can see a real doctor?"

Callie grinned. "Mak is a real doctor and I trust him completely." She coughed again, rolled on her side, and water ran from her mouth.

"He called his dad," Rowdy said as he pulled tissues from

a box on the counter and put them to her mouth, "and he's on his way out here to take a look at you."

"That's good," she said, rolling back onto the pillow. "He's been my family doctor since the day I was born."

Mak returned and took X-rays. "I thought I told you not to cross Lucas, Callie," the vet scolded. "He's still ticked that you made him move back into the bunkhouse after he had the run of the big house for almost a year."

Callie snorted. "Well, I went over the books he kept while holed up in my house, and I'm pretty certain he was skimming from the sales of cattle and horses, so I fired his ass and told him to stay off Miller Ranch or I'd have him arrested."

Mak shook his head and rolled his eyes. "And now he's tried to kill you."

Callie rubbed at her bruised eye. "I don't think a black eye is going to kill me." She stared from Mak to Rowdy. "Unless there's something you're not telling me."

Rowdy cleared his throat. "Somebody cut your brake line, Callie. Your accident was no accident," he said. "Someone tried to kill you and everyone in that bar last night heard Lucas Jones threaten your life."

"Oh, my god," Callie said with her hand moving to her mouth. "I can't believe the bastard would actually try to kill me."

"Who gets the ranch if you die, Callie?" Mak asked.

"What?" Callie asked with her eyes wide.

"Did you have to make a will when you joined MET and went out of the country?" Rowdy asked.

"Mom and Dad were still alive then," she said with a sigh, "so everything would have gone to them."

"And should they have died before you?" Rowdy asked. "The military always made us put in other contingencies. I can only assume MET does as well. Who did you name as the alternate to your parents to inherit this ranch?"

"I named you, Mak," she said, staring at the vet. "You're

the only person I could think of at the time who I knew would look after things."

Rowdy grinned at the astonished doctor. "Well, I think we can rule the good doctor out, so we're back to Lucas Jones or one of his cronies from the bar last night."

❧ 6 ❧

Callie spent three days in Mak's clinic. The X-rays showed she had a cracked eye socket from Lucas's punch, a broken nose from the airbag, and nothing more than the bruise from his vicious kick. "We got your Escape out of the ditch," Rowdy told her on his daily visit. "I had them haul it to the sheriff's impound yard," he told her. "I wanted to make certain their techs had a look at it."

"You're sure the brake line was cut?" Callie asked uneasily as she sucked on a popsicle.

"I climbed up and had a close look at it before the wrecker got there," Rowdy said with a nod.

Callie ran her hand through her matted red curls. "I guess I was lucky you decided to follow me that day."

"I followed you," Rowdy said, "because I saw a spot under where your truck was sitting and smelled it. Brake fluid smells like brake fluid and nothing else."

Mak walked in then, leading a small calf. "I brought someone in for a visit," he said, with a broad smile on his face and a large bottle of milk with a red nipple on it in his hand.

Callie's face lit up at the sight of the calf. "Oh, she looks so good, Mak."

Mak dropped her lead and the calf made its way around the bed to Rowdy, who petted it and laughed when it began to lick him.

Callie laughed as well. "I think she likes you, Mr. Waters."

"I guess it's my natural magnetism," Rowdy said with a chuckle. "Animals always like me."

As they were laughing and chatting about the calf, the sheriff Wallace Harris arrived. "I was sorry to hear about your accident, Miss Callie," said the heavyset man in his late fifties who reminded Rowdy of Boss Hogg.

"Did your techs have a look at her truck, sheriff?" Rowdy asked. "It was no accident, sir. Somebody cut that brake line and tried to kill Callie."

"Did you talk to Lucas Jones, Harris?" Mak asked, "or anybody who was at the Den the night he attacked her and threatened to kill her?"

"Now," the sheriff said, raising a pudgy hand to stop him, "my guy at the office said that brake line could have been snapped by hittin' a sharp rock on the road, so that's totally inconclusive and I have to classify Miss Callie's accident as just that, an accident and nothing more."

"And the brake fluid I saw pooled in the parking lot of The Devil's Den?" Rowdy asked with irritation edging into his tone.

The sheriff shrugged. "She likely hit something on the way into town that night and the fluid all ran out while she was parked." He smiled at Rowdy and arched a brow. "I understand she went home to spend the night with you?"

"I took her home with me to get her away from Lucas Jones," Rowdy growled in reply.

"I talked to Luke," the sheriff said, "and he's a mite riled about Miss Callie here firin' him without cause in front of everyone in the Den that night." He turned to Callie. "That wasn't very professional of you, Miss Callie, and Luke has every reason to be ticked in my way of thinkin'."

"I have plenty of cause, sheriff," Callie said. "I went through the books and I'm pretty certain Lucas was skimming from ranch sales in my absence." She glared at the sneering sheriff. "You're more than welcome to come up to the house after I get back home and go through them with me."

"I ain't no accountant, Miss Callie, and neither are you, but if you're open to it, I'll bring Calvin Hawks up with me from the tax office and he can go over it all with me."

Rowdy bent to whisper into Callie's ear. "I don't trust this guy, Callie. Take those books to a real professional before you let him, and his tax man get their hands on them."

Callie nodded. "I will," she whispered.

The sheriff cleared his throat. "Firin' Luke like that in front of half the town wasn't right, Miss Callie, and in his mind, he has almost more right to be there in that big house on Miller Ranch than you."

Callie's face turned beet-red. "This ranch is mine, sheriff, and Lucas Jones has no rights to it in any way."

The sheriff smiled. "His daddy was your grandpa's just like your daddy was, so I'd say he has a birthright of some sort."

Callie's mouth fell open. "The big difference," Callie said, collecting herself, "was that my daddy was born to the woman legally married to my grandpa. Lucas's mama was some two-bit bar trash who spread her legs for him and got knocked up." Callie pushed the blanket off and stood. "Lucas Jones has no legal standing as far as Miller Ranch is concerned and if he wants to get a lawyer and take me to court, then that's fine with me. I have my grandparents' marriage license, my daddy's birth certificate, and plenty of money in the bank for better lawyers. Tell my bastard uncle, if that's what he is, to bring it on. I'm more than ready for him."

The sheriff raised a brow. "I'm sure Luke will give you a run for your money, Miss Miller. He may have been born on the wrong side of the sheets, but in these days of liberal thinking, he might end up with a judge who sees and appreciates his side of the story."

"Then you're not going to do anything about his physical assault on her?" Rowdy demanded.

The sheriff smiled at Rowdy. "I talked to folks who were in the Den that night and from what I can gather, this little hellcat gave as good as she got, and probably deserved exactly what Luke gave her."

"Oh, come on," Rowdy snarled, jumping to his feet and startling the calf he'd been feeding from the bottle Mak had given him, "he punched her and then kicked the shit out of her while she was down and unconscious." Rowdy took a step toward the sheriff, pointing his finger and shaking it. "How do you figure she got what she deserved? I was there and saw the whole thing. Lucas Jones sucker-punched her and then kicked her while she was passed out on the floor." He glanced at Callie who stood shaking with rage. "How do you figure that was a fair fight. And what kind of man punches and kicks a woman like that anyhow?"

The sheriff returned his hat to his balding head. "I'd reckon it's a man fighting for what he feels is his," the sheriff said as he left the room and slammed the outside door.

"Well, I gather that didn't go well," Mak said. "Maybe I shouldn't have called him after all."

"If you hadn't," Rowdy said, "I was going to."

"For all the good it did," Callie snorted. "That asshole was certainly on Lucas's side in all of this and has no intention of charging him with anything."

"You can say that again," Rowdy snarled. "I'm surprised he didn't bust you for something."

Mak cleared his throat. "I should have anticipated that," he said with his face turning pale. "His and Lucas's mama are sisters, I think."

"Oh, my lord," Callie sighed. "I suppose I can forget about any sort of justice from him."

Rowdy snorted. "There's still the State Police and I'm calling them as soon as I get home."

They heard a loud bawling from the rear of the building that sounded like Maaa, Maaa, Maaa.

Mak began to laugh. "It sounds like I finally found someone to bond with our calf. I've been trying ever since you brought her in, Callie, but she's been having none of it," he said, grinning at Rowdy, "until now." The blond vet left the room giggling.

"What's he mean by that?" Rowdy asked Callie, who sat up on her pillows grinning at him.

"Since the calf lost her mother," Callie explained between giggles, "she needs to accept another to feed her." Mak led the calf into the room and it charged on unsteady legs for Rowdy and began to butt its head into his legs. "Looks like you're the lucky winner, big fella," Callie said laughing though it hurt her aching head.

Rowdy took the warmed bottle of milk from Mak and offered it to the calf who accepted the nipple and sucked with vigor. "Well, what do you know about that?" he said with an embarrassed smile on his suntanned face. "I can't wait to tell my mama that I'm a mama now too."

"I'm sure she'll be pleased," Callie said with a wink at Mak. "How often is he gonna need to come down here and nurse her, Mak?"

The vet smiled. "No more than six or eight times throughout the day until we can get her to begin grazing some." He laughed at the stricken look on Rowdy's face. Then he turned to Callie. "I fixed her hip as best I could," he said, "but I fear she's going to walk with a limp for the rest of her life and will likely never be able to run with a herd."

"Oh," Callie said with a sad glance at the nursing calf.

"What does that mean?" Rowdy asked, glancing up in confusion.

"It means she'll probably get picked off by a hungry wolf,

coyote, or cougar," Mak said. "Putting her down now would probably be the humane thing to do."

Rowdy's mouth fell open in shock as he went down on his knees and pulled the animal closer. "Are you really going to let him do that?" he demanded of Callie. "She's just a baby and has every right to live out her life."

"Mak's right, Rowdy," Callie said, defending the vet, "if we put her out with the herd, she'll just attract predators that would give her a horrible death and I can't afford to bring predatory animals close to the herds. It wouldn't be good business."

"I'll go get a shot ready," Mak said, "and we can send her on her way amongst friends with her belly full."

Rowdy took the bottle from the calf and wrapped his arms around it. "Don't let him do this, Callie. So what if she's a little crippled and can't run with the big herd? Raise her in the barn or a stock pen." He petted the calf's head. "I came back crippled from Afghanistan," he said and kissed the top of the animal's furry black head, "but they didn't give me any night-night shot to send me on my merry way to the afterlife."

Callie lifted her stump and glared at Mak. "You think I need one of those shots too, Mak?"

"Of course not, Callie, but you're not an injured calf who needs the protection of a herd to survive."

"I'll be her damned herd," Rowdy blurted out. "I'll take her up the mountain with me and raise her in the stable up there." He smiled at Callie. "She can keep me company while I'm working, and I won't have to pretend I'm not talking to myself all the time." He turned to Mak. "Will she give milk eventually?"

Mak raised a brow and glanced at Callie. "In a year or two after she's been bred and has a calf herself."

"Then that cinches it," Rowdy said with a grin. "I need a milk cow on my little farm to go along with my chickens." He kissed the little calf on the top of its head. "What ya say,

Princess? You want to blow this big bad ranch and go live with me and my chickens up on the mountain?"

The calf butted Rowdy's leg and bawled. Maaa.

"I suppose that says it all," Mak said, laughing. "If Callie is all right with it, then I guess you're the proud mama of a calf, Mr. Waters." He glanced at Callie, who nodded her approval. "Then come on back here with me and I'll give you the crash course on the care and feeding of a newborn calf."

The two men departed her room, leaving Callie alone with the calf. "It looks like you came out on top in this deal, little Princess," she said, scratching the calf between the ears as she stared at the empty doorway. "Maybe someday I'll be so lucky."

Rowdy Waters had probably saved her life twice now and he'd definitely saved the life of this sweet little calf. Had she really been that wrong about him? And look what he'd done with her family cabin since moving in. It had stood there for over a century and a half without running water or indoor plumbing. Now it had both in a manner of speaking. Callie couldn't wait to see what he did with it in the months to come. She smiled to herself, thinking of her grandmother and how delighted she'd have been to see those red gingham curtains on the windows.

Callie rubbed at the stump of her wrist. Losing her hand hadn't been Rowdy Water and the 107th's fault. It had been that damned Al-Sadi's and likely hers for wearing her great grandmother's emerald ring into a war zone. Al-Sadi had wanted that ring and when Callie had refused to give it up, he'd taken her hand and the precious family heirloom along with it. How could she possibly blame Rowdy for that?

❧ 7 ❧

Mak drove Callie up to the house when he and his father felt she was well enough to be released.

"Did you know Lucas Jones was my daddy's half-brother?" Callie asked Mak when he parked at the front door.

"Everybody knew, Callie," Mak said uneasily. "It was a pretty open secret around Miller's Crossing."

"I guess everybody except me," Callie said as she got out of the car. "Thanks for everything, Mak, but I'm sure glad to be back home again."

The first thing she did was run a hot bath in the big tub in her parents' room and soaked her stiff body for almost an hour.

"It's time you moved into this room, Miss Callie," Rita, the family's petite, Cheyenne housekeeper of twenty years or more said as she stripped the bed. "I'll put all fresh clean bedding on here to get the scent of that nasty Mr. Jones off everything. I already wash the walls, the windows, and the floors for you." She snorted as only Rita could to express her disdain. "That man is filthy and nasty, Miss Callie. You did right to fire him the way he put hands on young Zena in the kitchen and expected her to warm his bed like a common Tijuana whore."

"He what?" Callie gasped as she toweled herself dry.

"He's a nasty bad man, Miss Callie and me and Zena are glad to have him gone from this house."

"Well, he's gone for good, Rita, and you and Zena will only have to cook and clean for me now." Callie hugged the woman and kissed the top of her graying black head. "Do you really think I should move my things in here?"

"This room has been the room of the misters and mistresses of this ranch for as long as it's been a ranch," Rita said, "and now you're the mistress here, so yes, you should move from the little daughter's room into the Mistress's room." She nodded at a door across the room. "You should be in the room with access to the ranch office anyhow, so you don't have to be creepin' about in the dark hallways when you want to check on something in the records in the middle of the night."

Callie smiled. Her father had a terrible habit of thinking of something in the middle of the night and then jumping out of bed to spend hours in his office.

Callie's eyes went wide when Rita slid a large, gleaming Bowie knife from between the mattress and box springs on her mother's side of the bed and dropped it on the nightstand. "What the hell is that?" Callie demanded as Rita went on about changing the sheets and pillowcases.

Rita glanced back over her shoulder. "Miss Rachel tell me it for protection," she said with a grin. "I guess because of Mr. Morgan being away from home at night so much on his business trips in those last years." Rita finished making the bed and returned the knife. "I put it back for your protection now, Miss Callie."

Callie hugged the oversized white bath sheet tighter around her shivering body as Rita went to the walk-in closet and opened the door. "Where are my parents' things?" she asked, staring at the rows of empty hangers.

After the funeral and before that nasty man move in here, Zena and I folded all their things into trunks and took them to the attic," Rita said. "And even though that nasty man said you was dead in the desert somewhere with vultures picking at your carcass, we don't pack your things into trunks." She shook her head. "Packing things away is only for after proper funerals with the blessings of a priest to send the soul on to heaven, not before." Rita smiled and hugged Callie. "And here you are back at home alive and well where you belong. That nasty Lucas Jones is nothing but a greedy fool."

Callie opened her mouth to ask a question but didn't know whether she should drag the old housekeeper into her feud with Lucas or not. She shrugged mentally. Why the hell not? If anyone could tell her about shady goings-on where Lucas Jones was concerned, it would be Rita.

"I was looking over the books," Callie said, "and I think Lucas was stealing from the ranch funds after Daddy and Mama died."

Rita snorted again. "Don't surprise me none," she said.

With her interest peaked Callie asked, "How so?"

"Well," Rita said, running a hand through her short dark curls, "Mr. Morgan he always gives me a thousand dollars to buy groceries and such every month, but Mr. Lucas he tells me to tighten my bootlaces and only give me five hundred." She pursed her lips. "You know I always make a big nice supper for the boys in the bunkhouse on Sundays, but he tells me they can fend for themselves on Sundays and only to cook for him."

Callie scurried into the office and returned with the most current ledger in her hand. She ran a finger down the pages and saw that Lucas had indeed noted monthly cash advances to Rita of one thousand dollars and not five hundred. She'd been right. He was a thief and had been skimming money from the accounts. Now she had proof and a witness to back up her hunch. She also intended to do further investigations into those cattle and horse sales noted in the ledgers.

Tears stung Callie's eyes as she stared around her parent's room. Could she really move in here and try to take their place? Rita wrapped her arms around Callie. "It's time for you to take that bull by the horns, Miss Callie," she said in a soft, grandmotherly voice. "You know your grandfather would expect nothing less from his little fireball."

Callie choked out a sob, remembering her grandpa calling her that as he taught her to ride. "I know, Rita, but I just don't know if I'm up to it." She lifted her red stump. "I'm not a whole woman anymore and can't even get into a saddle without falling on my ass."

Rita snorted a laugh. "And how many times did little fireball fall on her ass before she finally got into that saddle and rode that horse?"

"More than my ass cares to remember," Callie said with a giggle.

Rita hugged her tight. "You will ride again, Fireball," the housekeeper said, kissing Callie's cheeks and brushing away the tears, "and you will manage this ranch just the way Old Mr. Morgan and the younger Mr. Morgan taught you to. You are a Miller woman," she said sternly, "and it's always been the Miller women who were the backbone of this ranch, not those silly men who thought they were, but only made most of their decisions with that little head between their legs most days."

Callie stared at the little woman with wide eyes and her mouth open in surprise as she waited for the housekeeper to continue. "My people have worked on this ranch for almost as long as it's been here," Rita said with a wink, "and we've seen things nobody else around Miller's Crossing has seen." She touched Callie's wet red hair. "You have your mother's Irish blood running in your veins, and those folks from across the sea are some of the fiercest I've ever known." She smiled and patted Callie's cheek. "Now it is time for you to move your things into this room to take Miss Rachel's place here and be fierce. You must take the reins of Miller Ranch the way she always intended for you to do." Rita turned to leave the room.

"Thank you, Rita," Callie said, "and go back to making your big Sunday Suppers for the ranch. I'll bring you a check for a thousand dollars the next time I come down. I'm sure your kitchen is in serious need of restocking."

"Thank you, Miss Callie," Rita said with a broad smile that caused her big brown eyes to sparkle. "That nasty man raided my cabinets every night, I think." She left shaking her head and muttering in Cheyenne to herself.

Callie went to her room, dressed in jeans and a t-shirt, and began to gather things from her dresser and closet. Maybe Rita was right, and it was time for her to move out of her childhood room and take the room of the owner of Miller Ranch. The Irish in her blood boiled at the thought of Lucas Jones making himself at home in there and sleeping in the bed where her parents had slept. Callie smiled to herself as she remembered the look on Lucas's face when she'd fired him in front of everyone in The Devil's Den that night. The sheriff might think it unprofessional, but that look had been priceless, and Callie would carry it with her forever.

By late afternoon most of her things were in her new room and she only had one more box of minutia to carry in and store in the closet. Her mother had decorated the room tastefully and Callie didn't think her old posters of rock bands would fit in. As she sat on the floor of the closet, Callie spotted a little sliding door in the wall. She opened it and saw a dusty cardboard box inside. She slid the heavy box out into the closet and brushed away the film of white dust on the top. Her curiosity peaked Callie pried up the cardboard flaps to find a collection of books inside.

She took one out, opened it, and gasped. They weren't just

books. They were diaries—her mother's diaries. Callie wondered what could be in them that made her mother conceal them away in a hidden compartment in the closet. She picked up the box and carried it to the bed.

"Rita thinks you had something to teach me, Mama," Callie said, glancing up toward heaven. "If I read these, am I gonna learn a lesson?"

Callie hurried down to the kitchen with the check in her hand for Rita. She fixed herself a sandwich, added some chips to the plate, and poured herself a tall glass of root beer over ice to carry back up to her room.

Callie dumped the box of diaries on the bed and sorted through them to put them in order by date. The oldest was one written by a young Rachel in her college years before Callie was born. She opened it and began to read.

"Well, here I am in my final semester. I can't wait for it all to be over so I can get back to the Crossing and take over Daddy's store. Luke is still hounding me to marry him, but I'm not ready for that yet and his mother is absolutely unbearable. There's no way I can live with that horrid woman and her endless chain-smoking. Had drinks with Morgan Miller before I drove back here to Missoula and he's cute."

Callie sat stunned. Was her mother referring to Lucas Jones? Had she actually dated him before her father? She continued to read.

"Luke drove up here furious today. He found out I went out with Morgan before I came back to school and that he's been coming up to see me. Man was he mad. He called me a whore and I lost it. I told him that with his mother as an example, he should certainly recognize a whore when he saw one. The son-of-a-bitch hit me and then ripped off my new dress and screwed me right on my dorm room floor. I'm so done with him and told him so. I haven't given it up to Morgan yet, but maybe it's time now. He's so sweet. Nothing like that asshole Luke."

Callie put a hand to her mouth in shock. Lucas Jones had raped her mother. How could she have allowed him to be hired on the ranch after that? Callie gulped the icy root beer and continued to read. Most of what came next were rambling about her classes, assignments, and friends she hung out with.

"Well, I've missed two periods now. It's official. The son-of-a-bitch knocked me up. Guess I should go home and have Doc Woods do one of his D&Cs to get rid of it, but I've always been secretly Pro-Life while the other girls here on campus hold their Pro-Choice rallies and I attend just to fit in."

Lucas Jones got her mother pregnant. Callie couldn't believe what she was reading. At least she had the good sense to abort the abomination. The next entry was dated a few weeks later.

"I told Morgan we were having a baby and he is thrilled. I suppose I should feel bad about deceiving him, but I just can't bring myself to kill a child in my womb. Lucas always rants about being a Miller because old man Miller knocked Doris up with him, so this baby will have a good many Miller genes too. Luke even looks a little like Morgan. I think every- thing will be fine."

Callie swallowed hard and wished she had more root beer in her glass. She fell back on the pillow with tears stinging her eyes. How could her mother have done such a thing? Then it struck her like Lucas's punch in the face. That baby was her. Tears of rage and shame blurred her vision as she read on.

"We're planning a huge Christmas wedding on the Ranch and every- body will be there. Everybody but Lucas Jones that is. I hope I never lay eyes on that no-good, low- life bastard again for as long as I live. Daddy had promised me a trip to Europe after graduation but instead I'm getting married to Morgan Miller and having this baby."

Callie slammed the diary shut. "So that trip kicking around Europe you told me about, Mama, was a lie too? I never thought of you as a liar before, Mama," Callie wept, "but you were one of the best I've ever known. You lied to Daddy and you lied to me. Everything about my damned life is a lie."

Callie glanced over at the dresser where the wedding

portrait of Morgan and Rachel Miller sat. They both looked so happy. She studied her mother's mid-section beneath the stunning bouquet of ivory and burgundy roses. "I guess I'm in that picture too beneath all that antique ivory silk and lace, huh, Mama." She cried herself to sleep that night on her mother's pillow in the room that had once been hers. Who was she? Really? The name on her birth certificate read Callista Jane Miller, but Callie knew now that half her genes belonged to Lucas Jones. How was she going to live with that and run Miller Ranch?

❧ 8 ❧

The next morning Callie pled ill when she wandered down to breakfast. She drank a cup of Rita's coffee and had a slice of toast, but her stomach wasn't up for much more and all she really wanted to do was crawl back into bed and hide beneath the blankets. "Have you decided on a new foreman yet, Miss Callie?" Rita asked as she joined her at the round oak table.

"I've been giving it some thought," she said, knowing the housekeeper already had someone in mind for the job. "Who do you think would fit the bill, Rita?" she asked with a grin.

Rita cleared her throat. "It's not my place to say," she said, "but Zena's husband Cody has been with the ranch for some years now and knows this land like the back of his hand."

Callie nodded. Cody Jackson had been on the top of her list for Lucas's replacement. He was a good cowboy, got along well with the other hands, and could likely take Lucas's place easy enough. "Don't tell Zena," Callie said, patting the house-keeper's hand, "and I'll make the announcement at our re-established Ranch Supper on Sunday afternoon."

"That is nice, Miss Callie, but—"

"Yes?" Callie said, arching her brow. That 'but' always meant something with Rita.

Rita leaned in close. "Don't tell anyone, but Zena and Cody are expecting their first baby." She smiled at Callie and the young ranch owner knew the big shoe was about to drop. "Zena and her man live in a third-floor walk-up apartment in Miller's Crossing," Rita said with a furrow in her brow. "Would it not be better for a pregnant mama to be to have a nice place to live and rest here on the ranch with her foreman husband?"

Callie stared at the old housekeeper. What did Rita have in mind? Did she expect her to move Zena and Cody into the house here? "I don't think I know what you're suggesting, Rita. I can't exactly build them a house here on the ranch to live in and I can't move an employee into the house here with me. Look how that worked out with Lucas." Callie's stomach turned just saying the man's name out loud.

"Oh, no, no, Miss Callie you don't have to build them a house," Rita said waving her hands in front of her face. "You already have one built."

Callie shook her head and picked up her cup of coffee. "I don't think having my foreman and his pregnant wife living with me here in this house would look right, Rita."

Rita slapped her hand down on the top of the table. "Not this house, you fool girl," she snapped in a tone Callie knew well. It was the one Rita used to scold and reprimand her as a child. "Your old playhouse on the other side of the pool that just stands empty since old Miss Jane passed away."

"The carriage house?" Callie said in an almost whisper. After Morgan Miller Sr. had passed away, her grandmother had moved into the building that had been built by Callie's great-grandfather to house their fancy carriages at the turn of the century and where the stable master and his family had lived. Callie's great-grandmother had been the daughter of that stable master and her grandmother had spent most of her young life in that carriage house. It had been her choice to end her days there and Callie had spent many hours there with the old woman before she passed.

"But nobody has lived in the carriage house in ages, Rita. The last time I was in there the paper was falling off the walls and the floor upstairs was warped from a leak in the roof." She swallowed more coffee. "I don't even know if the plumbing and electric work anymore out there."

Rita smiled and patted Callie's hand. "I go there to get things from time to time," she said. "Your mother still used it for storing the decorations for parties and holidays. The lights work but your papa had the water turned off after his mama passed in there." She poured Callie another cup of coffee. "You just need to find a man who knows about fixing old places up," she said with a shrug of her shoulders, "to go in there and fix things up."

Callie smiled at the housekeeper who'd always known how to get what she wanted. Where was she supposed to find someone who knew how to renovate and repair old buildings? She closed her eyes and a vision of red gingham curtains on the windows of the family cabin rushed into her mind. Rowdy Waters? Would her renter up on the mountain be interested in coming down to the ranch and working on the carriage house?

Callie finished her coffee. There was only one way to find out. She returned to her new room, dressed in jeans and a sweater, and hurried down to the garage to start her mother's car. The electric-blue PT Cruiser convertible with mock wood panel sides hadn't been run since her mother's death, but with her Escape now in a salvage yard, Callie only had the Cruiser to drive. It wasn't a practical vehicle to drive on rutted ranch roads, but until Callie could bring herself to go into Missoula to look for a replacement for the Escape she'd loved so much, it would have to do.

The day was sunny and bright. Callie backed the car out

of the garage and hoped the drive would blow off the dust that had accumulated on the vehicle. The gas gauge read three quarters of a tank and Callie unlocked the latches to roll back the roof and enjoy the beautiful day.

As she drove away from the valley floor the scent of cattle and pastureland changed to that of the larch and pine of the mountains. Callie had always loved the drive up to the cabin with her eyes peeled for wildlife on the narrow road. The cabin had been her grandma's place of escape from the worries of the ranch and her marriage to Morgan Miller Sr. Until reading her mother's diaries, Callie had never understood the woman's pain over her husband's philandering.

It had broken Callie's heart to read that Morgan Miller Jr. hadn't been any better than his father in that regard. She could still see the passage in her mother's diary.

"Little Penny Thompson visited me today. She spent the first hour telling me all about how she was trying to gather up twenty thousand dollars to buy out her father's interest in the cafe at the truck stop and then she hit me with the big news. She's pregnant and it's Morgan's baby. It seems they've been getting it on for almost now. It started sometime after I lost the baby last winter when I fell on the ice. I knew he blamed me for losing his son like that, but I never thought he'd resort to his father's ways to punish me. But then I look at my beautiful Callie and think that maybe I deserve it. Morgan loves her so much I could never admit the truth.

I finally told Penny that if she went to see Doc Woods for a D&C I'd give her the twenty grand she needs to buy the cafe. She was fine with that and left me to ponder what I was going to say to Morgan."

Callie had laughed at the thought of Penny ever being called 'little Penny' but then flushed with anger when she realized the woman who'd chastised her for aborting the fetus of that rapist had aborted the fetus of her half brother or sister for twenty thousand dollars. She didn't know what she was going to say the next time she saw the woman. Maybe she'd just avoid the cafe for a while.

The cabin came into view and Callie slowed the car. She

saw Rowdy shirtless on the roof adjusting solar panels. In the grassy yard, the black calf cavorted, chasing a butterfly through the clover more like a puppy at play than a calf. When she got out of the car it ran to her and butted at her hip.

Rowdy laughed. "She wants you to scratch her ears or give her a treat," he called down as he began to mount the ladder. "Hey," he said as something in the distance caught his eye, "climb up here and take a look at this." He put a pair of binoculars to his eyes and studied something in the valley below.

Callie climbed the ladder one rung at a time, careful with only the one hand to steady herself. As she neared the top, Rowdy took hold of her shoulder and held her until she sat beside him on the soft cedar shingles. "What is it?"

He handed her the binoculars and pointed to the west end of the valley. "Does that look like the truck that ran you off the road?"

Callie put the cumbersome glasses to her eyes and did her best to adjust the focus. After a few minutes and some help from Rowdy, a white semi came into focus with a cattle trailer behind it. "It sure looks like it," she said, "but I can't quite make out the name on the door. Can you see it?" She handed the binoculars back to Rowdy.

"Looks like it says Free Wheeling Enterprises," he said as he hung them around his neck again and let the heavy glasses fall to rest upon his bare chest. "You ever heard of that outfit?"

Callie scratched her red head. "It sounds familiar, but it's been a while since I had anything to do with the business. Daddy and his foreman always handled the transports of cattle to and from the ranch. It may be one of the companies they used, but I'm not certain."

"I've seen that truck and a couple of others running the ranch roads in the valley since I've been working on the roof up here and on the barn," he said. "Sure seems like a lot of trucks moving animals to me. Is it sale season or something?"

Callie shook her head. "Not really," she said. "Most of the big auctions aren't for another month or so."

They made their way back down the ladder and were met by the calf, who butted her nose against first Callie's and then Rowdy's legs.

Callie patted the calf and laughed. "My lord, what have you been feeding her? Miracle Grow? She's twice the size she was when you brought her home."

"Just milk," he said as he dug into his pocket and pulled something out, "and these," he said, offering the calf butting at him a slice of dried apple. "She loves these damned things."

The calf took the slice of dried fruit and when she knew there would be no more offered, returned to chasing the butterfly.

"She looks happy," Callie said.

Rowdy nodded. "I'm glad you let me take her. She's a great companion," he said but rolled his eyes and laughed when the calf tripped herself up on his toolbox, dumping his tools on the ground, "but not much of a workmate." He rushed over to rescue his tools from the grass. "To what do I owe this visit, landlady? Did I miss my rent payment this month or something?"

"Not at all," she said, staring up at the newly installed solar panels and the satellite dish on the roof. "As a matter of fact, I'm beginning to think I'm the one who should be paying you to live here and not the other way around."

Rowdy arched his brow. "Excuse me?" He began to walk back to the cabin. "Come on in," he said, opening the door, "I want to see if these panels actually do what they're supposed to do. I just put them up and charged the batteries for a day."

They went inside and he flipped a switch on the wall. Callie gasped when lights came on to illuminate the room. "What do you think of the new cabinets?" he asked.

Callie stared in wonder at cabinets that had never been in the tiny kitchen area before. Where there had only been crude shelves to stack dishes and pots before were cabinets made from four-inch planks of wood, a new countertop, and gleaming white tiles as a backsplash over the sink. She saw lower cabinets as well that replaced the shelves hidden by an old curtain. "It's all so beautiful, Mr. Waters, but it must have cost you a fortune. I would never expect you to spend your money to rebuild my place like this. Your rental agreement was for repairs not remodeling."

Rowdy chuckled. "I'm a rooter and a picker, Miss Miller. I made the cabinets from pallets I picked up behind some stores. They only cost me what I spent on the hardware and varnish."

Callie walked over to run a hand over the smooth, sanded surface of the countertop. "And these tiles?" she asked. "Those must have cost you something."

"Left over from another project," he said with a grin and beckoned her toward the bedroom.

Callie followed and walked into a room completely transformed. He'd rearranged the furniture and where the wardrobe had once stood there was a white tile shower in the corner with dark Victorian-era styled fixtures and a lacy curtain. Beside the shower stood a white pedestal sink with matching fixtures and over the sink was a heavy oval mirror in a gilt frame. Curtains hung at the windows that matched the shower drape and Callie's breath was taken away. "Oh, my god, Mr. Waters, this is unbelievable," she said as tears stung her eyes. "My grandma would have just loved this."

"Did you notice the furniture in the other room?" he asked.

"No," she said, rushing back out into the main cabin to see what she'd missed, and she burst out in sobs as she saw a couch to match her grandma's vine wood chair in front of the fireplace where he'd mounted a flat-screen television. Her grandma's chair sat to the side of the fireplace and on the floor was the porch swing that had once graced the front porch. Callie remembered it breaking or something when she was around ten or eleven and disappearing from the porch.

"Where the hell did you find all of this?" she asked, wiping tears from her face. "Up in the loft of the stable," he said. "Most of it was just in pieces, but nothing a little time and some Gorilla Glue couldn't fix."

Callie took a deep breath. "All I can say, Mr. Waters, is you're definitely the man for the job I came up here to offer you."

"Job?" he asked, raising a brow. "What kind of job?"

"I'm hiring a new ranch foreman," she said.

Rowdy raised a hand as if to stop her. "I don't know anything about ranching, Miss Miller."

Callie began to laugh. "That's not the job I intended to offer you."

"Oh," he said with his cheeks turning red with embarrassment. "Then please go on and I'll shut my mouth until you've said what you came to say."

"There is an old carriage house on the ranch I'd like to offer this foreman and his wife to live in," Callie said, "but it's been sitting empty and unused except for storage for several years. "I need someone to go in, look it over, and give it a good fix-up. The new foreman's wife is expecting a baby and I'd like the house to be in good condition when they move in."

"And what would this job pay exactly?" Rowdy asked with an impish grin.

Callie stared around at the improvements he'd made in the cabin lit by the electric lights he'd accomplished with his solar panels and wondered if there was enough money in her accounts to hire this amazingly talented man. "What would you say to fifteen dollars an hour, a place to sleep down on the ranch while you're working, and all your meals in my kitchen?"

Rowdy smiled, got up, and went to the refrigerator where he took out two cold beers. "I'd say this calls for a celebratory drink, boss." He saluted her with one of the bottles before handing it to her. "Come on out back and see what else I found at the dump."

Callie smiled, took the offered beer, and followed Rowdy outside. The calf ran to join them, and Rowdy gave her the expected apple treat. "I'll have to come up here every day to feed Princess," he said, "gather my eggs, and see to my garden."

They passed the chicken coop where several hens and a rooster scratched in the dirt and then came to a healthy garden with tomato plants staked high and full of bright red fruit. There were also pepper plants, rows of sweet corn, and vines of cucumbers and melons.

"You're a gardener too?" Callie said in awe of the luscious plants.

Rowdy chuckled. "I grew up on a farm in Missouri," he said, "and I like to eat."

"My cook on the ranch, Rita, would sure get a kick out of this," Callie told him.

They passed a spot with stakes in the ground. "What's this going to be?"

"Greenhouse," he said with a smile. "Man's gotta eat in the winter too, ya know."

They turned the corner at the rear of the cabin and Rowdy moved ahead of Callie to go to a large wooden tub. "Now this has been my best find yet," he said as he dipped his hand into the water and pulled out something he stared at before dropping it back in. "Holding perfect at one-o-four," he said, "Would you care for a nice hot soak, Miss Miller?"

Callie walked over to stare down into the tub of steaming water. "You have a damned hot tub up here?"

Rowdy nodded. "Best score ever. It was in pieces and the heater was shot," he said with a shrug, "but I put it all back together in a couple of days and I have a perfectly good heater to run the water through." He nodded to the rebuilt hot water heater as he gulped some of his beer. "Care to join me for a dip?"

Callie dipped a finger into the hot water. "I'd love to, but I don't have a suit with me in the car."

"Nobody wears a suit in my hot tub, Miss Miller," he said and unzipped his jeans. "Oh, come on," he said when he saw her hesitation, "I've seen you naked at least twice before and nothing happened."

Callie rolled her eyes and slipped her sweater off over her head. Why not? "All right, Mr. Waters, I suppose turn-about is fair play. Let's see what you have under all that denim."

Callie kicked off her shoes, slid off her jeans, and watched Rowdy do the same. She hated to stare, but the man was built like a brick shit house and had a package any porn star would be proud to sport. She followed him into the tub, gasping at the temperature and he took her hand as she eased down into the hot water beside him.

Aroused by his muscular body, relaxed some by the beer she'd consumed, and heated by the water, Callie put an arm around the man, pulled him close and kissed him. "Maybe nothing happened the last times you saw me naked was because I was unconscious," she mumbled between kisses. "I'm not unconscious this time."

"Hmm," he mumbled in reply as his hands began to roam over her body in the water.

9

Callie woke in Rowdy's arms and the late afternoon sun shone through the lacy curtains on the bedroom window. Who couldn't adore a man who hung lace curtains on his windows? Who couldn't adore a man who'd made her body react the way Rowdy had? After the months of sexual torture from Al-Sadi, Callie thought she'd never be able to enjoy sex again, but this afternoon with Rowdy had been glorious and she'd experienced more than one explosive orgasm. "I need to get home," Callie whispered into his ear. "Rita will be worried."

"She lives there with you?" he asked in a groggy voice.

"Now that her kids are grown and gone and her husband passed away," Callie said as she untangled herself from him and rolled off the bed to find her clothes, "she stays at the house sometimes now that Lucas isn't there anymore."

"I'm glad you have someone there to keep an eye on things," he said. "I'm gonna go pull a few things from the garden for you to take home to her, so she won't be too upset with me for keeping you so late."

Callie grinned. "How did you know fresh produce was the way to that woman's heart?"

"Because she sounds a whole lot like my mama," Rowdy said as he zipped his jeans and hurried out of the room in his bare feet.

Rowdy left the cabin with a broad smile on his face. In all his imaginings about Callie Miller, it couldn't have been better than it had been in real life. The woman had come on to him as soon as they'd gotten into the hot tub and when his cock was about to explode, she'd taken his hand and led him out of the water and into the cabin. She'd been a demon in bed, and he'd ejaculated more that afternoon than he had in ages. How had he gotten so lucky?

She'd come to him with a job offer and he'd been thrilled. These last improvements had taken the bulk of his savings and now that he had the solar panels and batteries installed it was time to buy a freezer and start prepping for the winter months. He had some roosters and a few hens to slaughter, and his garden to prep. If he could manage a few grand from this job maybe he could even negotiate for a side of beef and a hog from one of the local slaughterhouses.

Rowdy found an old bushel basket in the barn and filled it with cucumbers, a variety of peppers, tomatoes, ears of corn, and some zucchini squash. He carried the basket to the car and put it in her front seat along with a smaller basket of a dozen fresh eggs. His hens had been very generous of late, but they were more than he would be able to eat, and he hated to see them go to waste. If this Rita could make use of them then Rowdy was happy for her to have them.

Callie ambled out to the car and wrapped her arms around Rowdy's neck. "Thanks for a lovely afternoon, Mr. Waters. You have no idea how much I needed that." She kissed him hard before releasing him and walking to the driver's side door.

He grinned. "You're not the only one," he said. "When do you want me to come down with my tools to have a look at this job you have for me?"

Today is Friday," she said. "How about you come down tomorrow if you have time to take a look at the carriage house and then stay the night and enjoy one of Rita's fantastic Sunday Suppers with the ranch hands and me." She grinned at the uncertain look on his face. "I'm going to announce my decision about the new foreman and would like to introduce you to Zena and Cody. They're the ones you'll be fixing up the carriage house for." Callie opened the door and was met by the aroma of fresh corn, tomatoes, and peppers. "Oh, my. Look at all of this."

Rowdy grinned. "It's a bribe for your mama, so she won't be too pissed at me for keeping you out so late this afternoon."

"My mama?" Callie said with visions of Rachel in her head before she realized he meant Rita. "Oh, yah," she said with a hesitant smile, "she'll love all of this that's for sure and I bet most of it will make it into Sunday's supper for the hands."

"Oh yah?" he asked, staring at the basket. "How many will there be at the table?"

Callie shrugged her shoulders as she made a mental count of the hands, their spouses, and children. "Probably about a dozen or so," she said. "Why?"

"Then let me get some more of that corn," he said, turning to rush back to the garden.

He returned a few minutes later with his arms full of green ears of corn. "I only put a dozen in that basket," he said with a smile as he deposited the ears in her back seat, "and one ear of corn on the cob is never enough in my humble opinion."

"I'll see you tomorrow, Mr. Waters," Callie said as she dropped into the seat of the PT, started the engine, and backed out onto the narrow road. He may have been with the 107th but that was all forgiven now. This man was an absolute treasure and she didn't know how she'd gotten so lucky.

The ride down the mountain was as pleasant as the ride

up and Callie felt relaxed when she pulled the PT into the garage. Rita met her at the door with a stern look on her face. "I've been worried, Miss Callie? Is your phone broken?"

"I'm sorry, Rita," she said lowering her eyes. "I should have called, but I went up the mountain to talk to Mr. Waters about working on the carriage house, and lost track of time." She walked to the other side of the car, opened the door and took out the heavy basket of vegetables. "He made me bring you these in way of apology," she said and handed Rita the basket of eggs.

"This man has a garden up there?" she gasped, craning her head to see if there was more in the car. "And a hen house?"

"There's more corn in the back seat," Callie said and watched Rita's smile widen. "I'll get it and bring it in."

She carried the corn in and found Rita already emptying the basket, sorting the bounty into piles on the kitchen counter. She put a large red chili pepper to her nose and inhaled. "Oh, Miss Callie," Rita gushed, "I have beef ribs in the freezer. I can make the red chili beef you like so much with this and fresh salsa if you will make your deviled eggs." Her hands fondled the large green squash "And with these, I'll make loaves of zucchini bread for dessert."

Callie smiled at the old woman's excitement over the fresh produce. "I'm sure all the boys are happy to know Sunday Suppers are back."

Rita nodded with a bright smile on her face. "I told Zena to tell Cody and let them all know to be up here at the house at one on Sunday. We will celebrate the departure of that terrible Mr. Lucas in style." She patted Callie's cheek. "I think I love this man Rowdy Waters when he saved you from that Lucas in the bar, and then he saved you from drowning in your car," Rita said, "but now I know I love him for sure now."

Callie smiled. "Well, you'll get to meet him tomorrow," she

said. "He's coming down to look at the carriage house to give me an idea of what needs to be done to it to put it back into livable condition."

"And he is good with that sort of thing?" the housekeeper asked as she put produce into the refrigerator.

"He's an absolute marvel," Callie said and went on to tell her all the things Rowdy had already done to improve the cabin. "Do you remember that old vine-wood furniture grandma loved?"

Rita nodded. "It sat right in that living room until your mama and daddy married and brought in their own furniture," she said with a sigh, "and then your grandpa took it all up the mountain. I can remember your grandma crying every time a piece of it broke and your grandpa told her he burned it."

"But he never burned it," Callie said. "He just put it all in the loft of the stable up there. Rowdy found it, pieced it all back together, made new cushion covers, and put it all back into the cabin. He even fixed the porch swing."

Rita's brown eyes brimmed with tears. "Now I know for certain I love that man, Miss Callie, and I know your grandmama would love him too." She brushed the tears from her eyes. "I will love him for her, but I'm sure she is looking down from heaven now and loving him for fixing her beloved furniture." She poured Callie a tall glass of root beer. "She told me her daddy bought that furniture from a gypsy tinker man who brought it all the way from the grapevine region of northern California where it was made back when they'd first moved into the carriage house."

Callie's mouth fell open. "I had no idea it was that old."

"It was the last thing she had of her mama and papa," Rita said, "and it's the reason old Mr. Morgan hated it so much. He said it reminded him of her humble roots as the daughter of a stable keeper and he wanted her to remember that she was the wife of a rich rancher."

Callie snorted. "Yah, a rich rancher who couldn't keep his dick at home and out of other women."

Rita nodded. "She and your mama too might have been better served marrying a poor man like I did. My George never strayed from my bed because he knew the law wouldn't give a shit if his wife cut off a poor man's straying cock the way they would a rich one."

"I can see his point," Callie said with a giggle. "I think I'll try to avoid rich men from here on out, so I'm not in an unhappy marriage like Mama and Grandma were." Callie rose and left Rita with her produce. Al-Sadi had been a rich man in Afghanistan and if all rich men were like him, her father, and her grandfather, then Callie would remain single or look for a poor man—maybe a poor man like Rowdy Waters.

❧

Lucas Jones sat in Jamison Wheeler's office with a glass of Jack Daniels over ice in his hand as he waited for the man across the desk from him to look up from his papers and speak. He'd been called into Wheeler's office the day before by his pretty secretary and didn't look forward to the meeting.

"How are things out in cow country, Jones? My trucks are rolling every day, but my quotas still aren't being met. I need to hit your big herd out there to keep up."

Lucas knew this was going to be the topic of conversation for this meeting and he already knew how he was going to play it. "Go ahead and start picking off cattle from the Miller herd, Mr. Wheeler."

Wheeler looked up with an arched brow. "Why the hell the change of heart now, Lucas?"

Lucas shrugged. "The bitch fired me from my position of twenty-five fucking years at that ranch," he said. "So pick off her damned herds, so I can show the court what a miserable excuse for a ranch owner she is when I sue her ass for my birthright."

"Your birthright?" Wheeler queried as he sipped his whiskey.

"My father was Morgan Miller Senior and my lawyer says I'm entitled to that ranch as much or more than that hateful little one-handed bitch is. I just have to prove to the court that I'm more capable of running it than she is."

"I gather that since your last name is Jones and not Miller your mother was not his legal wife," Wheeler smirked as he twirled the glass, listening to the ice cubes tinkle in the smooth Tennessee whiskey. "What makes you think any court is going to give you title to the property over the daughter of the legitimate heir?"

Lucas swallowed the last of the whiskey in his glass. "For one thing," he said with a snarl, "I have just as much Miller blood in my veins as she does and I'm a man who's overseen that damned ranch for almost as long as she's been alive." He raised his hands. "I'm a man and I still have both my hands so I can still ride with a herd and do the work required of a real ranchman." Lucas chuckled. "That fool bitch can't even manage to keep her car on the road."

"In other words," Wheeler sneered, "your little ploy to take her out of the picture permanently failed."

Lucas snorted. "Not on any account of mine," he said. "Her car flipped into a ditch, but some do-gooder stopped and dragged her out before she drowned." He refilled his glass. "If it comes down to it, I'll sneak into that big house and take her the way I did her bitch mother some years ago."

"Oh, yah?" Wheeler said, wondering at Lucas's boast now.

"I surprised the cunt one afternoon in the shower," he said, "and I grabbed her up, threw her over my shoulder, and carried her into the bedroom where I filled her cunt with my meat for over an hour while she squirmed and squealed, pretending she didn't enjoy every minute of it." Lucas chuck-led. "She was still the same horny bitch I screwed in high school and in need of a good dick between her thighs after living with that surly half-brother of mine for all those years." He winked at Wheeler. "I bet her red-headed cunt daughter has a pussy just as sweet and I think I'll get a taste of it before I do away with her for good."

Wheeler took a revolver from his desk drawer. "Perhaps you should try a more direct approach the next time."

"I'm gonna beat her ass in court," Lucas said as he stood, "so take all the cattle you want in small groups so the stupid cunt never notices they're missing until I demand a reckoning in court to prove she can't manage the business." He winked at Wheeler. "But when Miller Ranch is back in my hands, things go back to the way they were before."

Lucas left the office and Wheeler stared after him, running his hand over the barrel of the gun. "Or maybe I'll just have to take a more direct approach with you, Lucas. I really hate to suffer a disgusting piece of filth like you to live when I have daughters out there who might run afoul of you."

❧ 10 ❧

Rowdy arrived at Miller Ranch before noon on Saturday with his tools, a notebook, and something more for Rita in the back of the Cherokee. Callie and a petite dark-skinned older woman met him in the drive. As soon as he stepped out of the Jeep, the older woman rushed up to him with her arms wide. "You are such a good man, Mr. Rowdy," she said in a slightly accented voice as she wrapped her arms around him, and Callie stood back grinning.

"Thank you, ma'am," Rowdy said with his cheeks flaming red, "but isn't this a bit much for a few ears of corn and some tomatoes?" He winked at Callie. "Why don't you look in the back and see what I brought with me today?"

Rita glanced up at him and grinned before rushing to the back of the jeep and opening the door. "Oh, praise be to Jesus," she gasped as she rolled out a large watermelon and grasped cantaloupes in both her petite hands. "These will be perfect to cool the mouth after my red chili beef tomorrow." She smiled at Callie. "I'll ice them down and then use the melon baller to make pretty bowls for both ends of the table." She motioned for Rowdy and Callie to bring the melons inside the house."

"Now you've done it," Callie told him as she scooped cantaloupes into the tail of her long t-shirt. "If she doesn't drag a priest out here tomorrow to marry us, she'll probably drag you to church in the morning to marry you herself."

"You didn't tell her that you'd already deflowered me and I'm no longer suitable for a proper church wedding?" Rowdy asked with a grin.

Callie rolled her eyes as they walked toward the house. "Don't be ridiculous, Mr. Waters, I don't kiss and tell."

"This place looks a lot bigger down here than it does from up on the mountain," he said, staring at the tall white columns holding up the porch roof. "Sorta reminds me of Southfork on that old tv show about the Texas ranchers."

Callie giggled. "I think that's the exact effect my grandpa was going for when he added this to the house. My grandma hated it and called it gauche."

Rowdy smiled. "I think I'd have liked your grandma."

Callie kissed his cheek before they entered the house. "I'm sure she'd have liked you too."

They went into the kitchen and put the melons on the counter. "Are you hungry, Mr. Rowdy?" Rita asked. "I can make you a nice Bacon, lettuce, and tomato sandwich." She grinned up at him. "I have some beautiful tomato in my refrigerator now."

"Oh, no thank you, ma'am, I made myself a big pan of scrambled eggs for breakfast just before I drove down the mountain."

Callie took him by the arm. "We need to get out to the carriage house anyhow, Rita, if you want to have it ready for Zena and Cody to move into before that baby gets here."

"Shh," Rita shushed her in a scolding tone. "Nobody is supposed to know about the baby but me."

Rowdy made like a zipper across his lips. "I know nothing," he said with the accent used by an old television character as he grinned.

"Come on, you big suck-up," Callie said, pulling him toward the rear door.

"Wow," he gasped when he saw the huge pool and the patio furniture, "this looks like some sort of spa or resort."

"Yah," she said with a snort, "almost a tropical paradise except for the snowcapped mountains in the distance and the smell of cow shit on the breeze."

Rowdy grinned. "Well, there is that. Is this more of your grandfather's gauche doing?"

Callie shook her head. "No, this was all dear ol' mom," she said with a frown. "Her idea of rich was a cement pond in the back yard and not grass. Grandma liked having the pool, but she hated Mom's big pool parties and all the stuck-up snobs she invited to show it off to." Callie unhooked a gate and they walked along a stone path to the faded wooden structure in serious need of wood treatment or paint.

"Did you and your mother not get along?" Rowdy asked as he waited for Callie to open the door of the carriage house.

"Until just recently I thought the world of her," Callie said as they walked inside, and she flipped a switch to turn on a dim bulb.

Rowdy didn't push the subject when Callie said no more about her late mother. He saw a large fieldstone fireplace and walked over to examine it. "Do you know if this still works? I mean is the damper intact and functioning as it should?"

"I don't think so," she said. "The last time they lit it up after a party it smoked the place up pretty bad."

He took out his note pad and scribbled on it. "Would you like the outside wood stained and refinished or painted white to match the main house?"

"It's always been a nice warm wood color," she said, staring around the big living room area. "Let's keep it that way."

Rowdy nodded and scribbled something more. They walked into the spacious kitchen and Rowdy gasped. "That's one hell of a stove," he said, moving closer to the huge black iron cook stove with six gas burners and a wide copper hood in need of serious polishing. "You could get a fortune for this at a good auction."

Callie shook her head. "This ol' girl has been in here since just after the turn of the century when the new-fangled gas cook stoves came out on the market," she laughed, imitating her grandma. "We'll clean her up, make certain there are no leaks in the gas fittings, and leave her right here where she belongs."

Rowdy nodded. "It's why I left the old wood stove in the kitchen up on the mountain," he chuckled, "that and it would have broken my fucking back to drag it out to the barn."

By the time they made it through the bathroom, the downstairs bedroom where her grandmother had slept, and the two upstairs rooms filled with Rachel's party and holiday decorations, Rowdy had his notebook filled with mostly minor fixes. The wood floors need to be sanded and refinished on both levels and there had been a leak in the roof that soiled the ceiling in one of the upstairs bedrooms, though Callie thought the roof leak had been attended to some years ago.

"So do you think you can handle all of this, Mr. Waters?" Callie asked as they were leaving the carriage house.

"Once you get all the junk moved out, I can probably get it spiffed up in a week or so." He smiled at her frown. "You didn't expect me to haul out all that personal family stuff, did you?"

She returned his smile. "No, I suppose Rita and I can handle that. And the exterior?"

Rowdy stared up at the board and batten walls, silvered with age and lack of care. "I'll get up there and check the roof right away, but the staining and sealing I can do once your tenants move in. Let's get the inside dealt with first."

Callie wiped the dust from her hand on her jeans and realized that for the first time in weeks, she hadn't thought about her missing hand. She'd simply gone on about her life as though nothing had changed and she was just her old self again, attending to her life and the business of the ranch. Was that because of this man or had she begun to adjust to her new condition the way her therapist had told her she eventually would?

When they walked into the house, Callie heard Rita speaking sternly with someone in the front foyer—a male someone. She walked through the kitchen and into the living room to find the sheriff in his official uniform and hat standing over Rita with a scowl on his flushed face.

"May I help you, Sheriff?" Callie asked, uncertain how to address him after their last encounter.

"I have official papers to serve you with, Miss Callie," he said with an empty smile as he scowled back at Rita, "but this foul little gnome you have guarding your gate here wouldn't get you for me."

"Well, I'm here now." Callie smiled and winked at Rita. "You can go back to the kitchen now, Rita, I can take care of this from here."

Rita scowled back at the sheriff. "Yes, back in the kitchen where we foul gnomes keep our sharp knives to poke fat nasty men." She turned and stalked back to the kitchen.

Callie found it hard to suppress a giggle when she saw Rowdy smiling in the room behind her. "You have papers to serve me, Sheriff?" she said, straightening her face.

The sheriff handed her a folded set of papers. "You've been served, Miss Miller," he said with a self-satisfied grin on his pudgy face after she took the papers.

Callie waited for the man to leave and get in his county squad car before she unfolded the sheets of paper to inspect them. "Son-of-a-bitch," she growled when she saw the name on the top: Lucas (Miller) Jones vs Callista Miller in the matter of the title to Miller Ranch et all.

"What is it, Callie?" Rowdy asked after giving her a

moment. Rita now stood at his side with her arm around his waist like a worried little grandmother.

Callie refolded the papers and slapped them on her leg. "It seems Lucas is suing me for ownership of this ranch."

"What?" Rita gasped as she clung to Rowdy. "That nasty bastard boy of ol' Mr. Miller got no claim here and I told him so when he brought it up when he moved his greedy ass in here like he owned the place." She released Rowdy and stalked back into the kitchen muttering about bastards and nasty men.

"I'll take these into Missoula on Monday and give them to our lawyer," Callie said, tossing the bundled of legal papers onto a table. "He's kept on retainer to handle this sort of thing."

"There have been others?" Rowdy asked with an arched brow.

"My grandpa was a big screw around," she said with a sigh, "and so was my daddy, I guess. There have been others who came round with their hands out, looking for a payoff," Callie said, remembering her mother's diary entry about little Penny. She nodded to the papers. "Lucas just thinks he's entitled to a very big one." She took Rowdy's hand and they walked into the kitchen where Rita was still mumbling about bastards and nasty, no-good men.

"Oh, Mr. Rowdy," Rita said with tears in her big brown eyes, "you take care of my Miss Callie now, and save her from that nasty Mr. Lucas?" She wrapped her arms around Rowdy's waist and wept softly into his shirt.

Rowdy glanced, wide-eyed at Callie who stood at the refrigerator with two beers in her hand and smiled sympathetically at him.

He returned Rita's hug and stroked the old woman's hair as she clung to him. "I'll look after her, Rita," he said in a soft comforting voice. "Nobody is gonna hurt your girl as long as I'm around. I promise you that."

Callie's heart melted at the tone in his voice. Rita was nobody to him and he certainly didn't have to be comforting her this way. Wasn't this the sort of man she read about in those romance novels?

Rita lifted her head and stared up into Rowdy's face. "Thank you, Mr. Rowdy," she said with trembling lips. "Miss Callie is a good girl, but she's too headstrong for her own good sometimes and that Mr. Lucas hurt her once and maybe twice if he cut the brakes on her car like you think he did." She glanced at Callie. "I worry for that girl so much, Mr. Rowdy and she's all alone in this world now with her daddy and mama out back in the ground like they are with poor little Mr. William. At one time, I thought it would be Mr. Mak coming to take care of her but," Rita snorted and waved her hand in the air, "he too much a sissy boy with his pretty hair in a pony-tail, his earrings, and his pretty pink ties. She needs a strong man like you, Mr. Rowdy—a real man." Rita began to weep again and scurried off for the downstairs bathroom.

"Mak the vet?" Rowdy asked with his brow raised. "Should I be jealous?"

"We were sort of engaged once," she said, "but no if anything I should be the jealous one. Mak would be much more interested in sleeping with you than me."

"Oh," he said with his cheeks turning red, "I see."

Callie walked over and handed Rowdy one of the beers. "It seems my housekeeper has grown attached to you, Mr. Waters," she said with a grin.

"It's that natural magnetism I was telling you about," he said as he opened the beer and took a long swallow to calm his nerves.

"I thought you said it was animals that loved you?" Callie grinned.

"And fierce little gnomes, it seems," he replied, returning her grin.

❧ I I ❧

The return of Sunday Supper to Miller Ranch was a roaring success. Everyone loved Rita's red chili beef and Callie's deviled eggs. The long table set up on the patio beside the pool was dressed festively with the good family china, a large flower arrangement, and crystal bowls at each end filled with the colorful, sweet melon balls. The six hands who lived in the bunkhouse and the three who lived in town with wives or girlfriends all showed up dressed in their Sunday best for the occasion.

There were two barrels of ice for bottles of beer and cans of soda. When the plates of zucchini bread were passed around, Callie stood and tapped her fork on her bottle of beer.

"Thank you, Rita, for another wonderful meal." She clapped and everyone else did as well.

Rita stood. "You should all really be thanking Mr. Rowdy for all the beautiful tomatoes, chilis, and other things from his garden, including that beautiful sweet corn and the melons." She clapped and everyone else joined in.

Callie beamed at the table, thrilled to have all her employees together in one place enjoying a meal together.

Sunday Suppers on the ranch had been going on since before her great-grandfather's day. He knew it was a way to promote camaraderie amongst the hands and bring them and their families if they had them closer to their employer.

"I know you've all been at loose ends a bit since I dismissed Lucas Jones from his position as foreman."

There was some murmuring, but Callie didn't think it was murmurs of approval or on the side of Lucas. "I've spoken with all you men to get your opinions upon who you feel would be the best man to replace Lucas." There were more murmurs and the nodding of heads. "I've made my decision and I have to say, the decision was an easy one." She smiled at Cody Jackson who sat smiling at his wife, Zena and holding her hand. "Cody Jackson," Callie said in a louder voice, "will you stand, please?"

Cody released his wife's hand and stood. "Ma'am?" he said courteously.

Callie smiled at the forty-year-old cowboy who'd worked on Miller Ranch since he'd graduated from high school. "After long discussions with your co-workers and much thought, I've decided to offer you the Foreman position on Miller Ranch."

Cody's face brightened and his coworkers clapped around him. "Thank you, Miss Miller, I'd be honored to accept the position if," he said, glancing down at his wife, "Zena is all right with it."

"Of course, I'm all right with it, you big fool," she said with a grin on her pretty face.

"But it's gonna leave you home alone more and with ..." his voice trailed off and his face turned pale.

"I have a little something to sweeten the deal," Callie said with a quick glance at the smiling Rita. "Our foremen have always bunked with the hands in the bunkhouse if they didn't have a house in town or somewhere around with family," Callie said, "and I don't think that's always been comfortable or convenient, so I've decided to offer you the carriage house over there," she nodded at the structure on the other side of the pool, "as the new foreman's residence."

Cody returned to his seat beside his wife, who sat beaming with pride and anticipation as she turned to stare across the patio at the carriage house. "It's so big," she gasped, and no stairs to get to the front door.

Callie grinned. "Mr. Waters here," she said with a nod to Rowdy beside her has agreed to do a little fix up on it and says he'll have the inside ready for you to move into in a week or so and then he's going to restain and finish the siding on the outside."

Rowdy stood and offered his hand to Zena. "Me and Miss Callie have the upstairs rooms cleaned out now and I'd like to get an idea about what colors you'd like the walls painted. Would you mind coming over with me to do a walkthrough and tell me what you think you'd like along those lines?"

Zena glanced up at her husband and then to Callie. "I get to choose the paint colors?" she asked in surprise.

"You're the one who's going to be living there, not me," Callie said with a grin. "You and Cody go ahead over with Rowdy and tell him what you'd like, and I'll make certain you don't end up with something weird."

Cody laughed as he stood. "Maybe I like weird," he said.

"That's why I asked your wife to choose and not you," Rowdy said as he left the table with Zena's hand still in his.

"Oh, Miss Callie," Rita said as she joined Callie at the table, dropping down into Rowdy's vacant chair, "Zena looks so happy."

"Everyone looks happy, Rita," Callie said, taking the old woman's hand. "It was a fine meal and I think everyone had a great time. I think they're glad things are going back to normal around here."

Rita rolled her eyes. "Now that nasty Mr. Lucas is gone."

Callie kissed the top of the housekeeper's head. "Indeed," she said. "He's gone and he won't be back."

Rita nodded and grinned. "I see you put Mr. Rowdy in your old room," she said and then lifted one of her dark brows, "but it looked like he may have ended his night joining you in yours."

Callie smiled. "He said the tv stopped working."

"Uh-huh," Rita said and walked away toward the kitchen giggling.

She and Rowdy had spent an enjoyable night together and Rita wasn't going to make her feel guilty about it. She was an adult now and this was her house. If she wanted to enjoy the company of a man in her room, nobody had the right to tell her she couldn't. She got up, went to the barrel of ice and fished out a bottle of Bud.

An hour after leaving the patio Rowdy returned to her side along with the others. "It looks like I'm going to have a lot of painting to do. Miss Zena wants a different color scheme in every room," he said rolling his eyes.

"They all needed fresh paint," Callie said. "The place has sat empty since Grandma died over ten years ago."

Cody walked up with Zena and two of the hands and slapped Rowdy's back. "This fella's gonna give that kitchen a complete upgrade with new cabinets," he said, smiling.

"And we're the ones who have to run around and gather up pallets from behind the stores," one of the hands complained good-naturedly, "and then take 'em apart."

"And I promised you beer," Cody countered with a wink at Callie. "I made most of our furniture from reclaimed pallets," he said. "Zena bought me a book our first Christmas together with a ton of plans and ideas in it, but I never imagined kitchen cabinets."

"You should have him take you up to the cabin he's renting to show you what he's done up there," Callie said. "He's a real miracle worker with old buildings."

"I'd love to see it," Zena said excitedly. "I love seeing new ideas."

Rowdy's face turned red with embarrassment. "It's not really all that much," he said, kicking at a rock on the ground. But maybe one of those trucks will be buzzin' around for you to get a gander at," he said to Cody.

At the mention of the truck, Callie's head came up. "Is Free Wheeling Enterprises a company we do business with, Cody?" she asked her new foreman. "If they were, they aren't anymore. I'll not do business with a company that runs up and down ranch roads where there is open range the way that truck was that hit me and probably hit that cow of ours."

"I've seen the trucks around a lot of late," Cody said, glancing toward the road, "but they're not a company Miller Ranch has ever done business with to my knowledge, Miss Callie. We've used Piper's for transport for as long as I've been here."

"Good," she snorted, "and we never will use Free Wheeling."

"Yes, ma'am," Cody said with a nod.

Cody, Zena, and the others walked away to mingle with the other hands, leaving Rowdy and Callie standing alone.

"So, what do you plan to do with the rest of your evening?" Rowdy asked. "Would you be interested in joining me for dinner at Penny's?"

Callie put her hand to her belly and rolled her eyes. "I'm still so stuffed I can't think about food," she said with a grin. "We usually just munch on leftovers out of the fridge on nights after one of Rita's Sunday Suppers. Anyhow, I think Penny closes up at five on Sundays." She smiled at him and took his hand. "How 'bout you veg here with me tonight and watch tv on the couch in the living room. We'll finish up what's left in the refrigerator and go out tomorrow night."

Rowdy put his hand to his mouth and belched. "Good idea," he said. "I'm gonna run up the mountain and feed Princess. I'll see if Cody and Zena want to come along to see the cabinets I did up there."

Callie grinned. She knew he wanted to show off everything he'd done up there and well he should.

She watched Rowdy, Zena, and Cody leave, chatting excitedly about the improvements to be made on the carriage house as they walked. Callie wondered if she'd ever be excited like that about moving into a new place. She glanced up at the big ranch house. No, this was her place now and she didn't see herself moving anyplace else anytime soon. Miller Ranch was her future now.

She joined Rita in the kitchen and helped her to deal with the leftovers and the dishes. "It was a great success, Rita," Callie said, hugging the petite housekeeper. "I think everyone is thrilled to have our Sunday Suppers back."

"And I am so happy you are giving my niece and her husband that house to live in," Rita said, returning the hug. "With the baby coming, it will be good to have her close and not having to climb all those stairs in Miller's Crossing."

"Having a separate residence for my foreman is something we should have done long ago," Callie said with a sigh. "It might have put an end to some of this trouble before it ever got started," she said as she arranged clean dishes in the china hutch.

Rita snorted. "That Mr. Lucas was going to cause trouble no matter what you'd done, Miss Callie," the housekeeper said. "He always been a bad man."

"Did you work at the ranch when Lucas started here?" Callie asked.

"Old Mr. Morgan brought him here," Rita said, nodding, "even though he knew it would hurt your grandma to see him strutting around like a banty rooster as though he owned the place." She shook her head. "That man had a mean streak too, making your sweet grandma live here and see the child he'd fathered upon another woman like that."

"Grandma just let him bring Lucas here and put him to work?" Callie asked in surprise. It stunned her some that Jane

Miller would put up with that sort of treatment from her husband.

Rita shrugged. "Where was she gonna go? She grew up in that carriage house over there. This ranch was all she'd ever known and by then, her parents were gone. All Miss Jane had was this ranch, your grandpa, and your daddy, so she swallowed her pride and put up with having Lucas around." Rita grinned. "It was Doris coming around where Miss Jane finally put her foot down and said, 'no more.'

Callie's mouth fell open. "Lucas's mother was coming out here too?"

Rita snorted again. "That floozie would show up here and sneak into the carriage house to wait for your grandpa to show up for her to entertain." Rita began to laugh. "You shoulda heard the hullabaloo when your grandma showed up with her sawed-off shotgun in hand and told her in no uncertain terms to get her skank ass off Miller Ranch and never come back."

Callie began to laugh along with Rita. "Now that sounds more like the grandma I remember."

"Your grandma even pointed that gun at your grandpa when he tried to come between her and Doris," Rita said with a grin. "She screamed like a banshee and came close to pulling the trigger."

"But she didn't did she?" Callie said with a sigh. "I dare say the Miller family would have been better off if she had."

Rita smiled. "Your grandma loved your grandpa very much, Miss Callie, and she'd never have hurt him."

"It sounds like he didn't mind hurting her, though," Callie said. "Did he?"

"He did seem to enjoy tormenting the poor soul," Rita said, "with his women and his sexual depravities." Rita shook her dark, graying head. "Poor Miss Jane didn't deserve that. She was a fine woman and always treated us who worked in the house with respect and kindness." She hugged Callie. "Just like you do, Miss Callie."

❧ 12 ❧

Work began in earnest on the carriage house the following day. Rowdy rented a floor sander from the Ace Hardware and along with Callie, they sanded and then varnished the old hardwood floors. The varnish caused colors to pop in the wood Callie had never seen before.

Around noon, the sound of hammers deconstructing pallets came from outside and boards piled up that would become cabinets soon. Rowdy and Cody went over plans Rowdy had sketched and before they called it a day, they had the next day's work planned out. Callie and Zena washed windows on both floors as Zena told her about plans to paint the walls and decorate the nursery. Callie hoped to someday have this much enthusiasm for wall colors and curtains. She supposed conceiving a child with the man you loved was much different than the way her child had been conceived. Jealousy stabbed at her heart and Callie did her best to fight the feeling. She heard Rowdy and Cody laughing about something downstairs. Was Rowdy Waters a man she could see having a life with? Sharing a child with? Callie shook off the thought. Rowdy Waters was a distraction and an employee.

"I don't know about you, Miss Callie," Rowdy said when

she made her way downstairs, "but I'm about ready for a hot shower and that dinner at Penny's. How about you?"

Callie grinned. "I don't know about Penny's food," she said as she stretched, "but that hot shower sounds good."

"We're gonna start movin' some stuff in tonight if that's all right," Cody said. "Zena is eager to be out of that damned apartment."

"You have the keys," Callie said and motioned around the room with her hand. "This is your place now, Mr. Foreman, move in whenever you want."

Cody smiled as he took his wife's hand. "You have no idea how good that sounds, Miss Callie. Being foreman on Miller Ranch has been a dream of mine for a long time now. Thank you."

"Don't be ridiculous, Cody," Callie said. "I'm the lucky one here. Miller Ranch is lucky to have a man like you to fall back on as foreman."

Cody's face flushed. "Aww, I don't know about that, Miss Callie."

Rowdy stepped in and took her arm. "Let's go and get that dinner so these two can get back to work, Callie."

"Yah, a burger and fries are beginning to sound good," she said, "but I need to shower some of this sawdust off my body first."

"I told you sanding these floors was gonna be a big job," Rowdy said with a wink at Cody.

"Yah," the foreman said, "but they really look great. Thanks."

Callie showered and dressed in her good jeans and a flannel shirt. She had better clothes, but they were only going to Penny's for a burger. Denim and flannel would suit for that. Callie was still irritated with the sanctimonious woman and didn't know what she'd say if Penny hassled her about aborting Al-Asadi's baby again. What Callie did with her body was her business and not Penny's.

In a foul mood, Callie didn't make much conversation on their way to the cafe, and Rowdy gave her space after trying to start a conversation twice and being shut down. The sun was setting behind the mountains when Rowdy parked his Jeep in the gravel lot, got out, and opened the door for Callie.

"I'm sorry if I did something to upset you, Callie," Rowdy said as he opened the door for her to enter.

"I'm just really tired," she said and yawned as they took seats at an empty corner table. "Maybe we should have put this dinner off until we had the carriage house a little closer to finished."

"What," he said with a grin, "and screwed up my therapy schedule?"

Callie furrowed her brow. "Your therapy schedule?"

The waitress brought them water and menus. Rowdy opened the menu. "Yah, my therapist at the VA gave me a sheet of tasks to perform before my next session with the new doc in Missoula," he said, and taking a member of the opposite sex out for a meal was the last thing on the list."

"Is that so?" Callie fumed, "and where on the list was getting a woman into bed for the afternoon?"

"Nowhere," Rowdy said in sudden confusion at her temper. "I mean that wasn't on the list." He put the menu down. "Look, I—"

"I think it would be best if you just took me back home, Mr. Waters. You can take this off your damned list, but I'm really not in the mood to be your therapy project for the evening." Callie pushed the chair back, stood, and marched out the door.

"Sorry," Rowdy told the waitress as he dropped three dollars on the table, "the lady changed her mind about dinner."

They didn't exchange two words on the way home and when he stopped the Cherokee in front of the ranch house,

Callie jumped out, marched to the door, and slammed it when she went inside.

Rowdy just sat there with his chin on his chest. What had just happened? What had he done to get her into such a mood? He flinched when someone tapped on the car's window. It was Mak and Rowdy rolled the window down.

"Pete and I were just going out for a little walk when we saw you drive up," Mak said. "I gather your date didn't go well?" he said with a grin.

"You guys dated for a while?" Rowdy asked.

Mak snorted. "You could sorta say that," he said. "Technically we were engaged."

"You were in love with her then?"

"I love Callie like the sister I never had," Mak said, "but I'm not in love with her. I'm not exactly the kind of man who'd be in love with Callie Miller or any woman," he said with a raised brow, "if you get my meaning?"

"You're gay?" Rowdy asked.

Mak chuckled. "As a three dollar bill," he said.

❧

Callie stormed up the stairs. Was she just his therapy project? Someone he'd settled on to please his therapist. How could she have been so gullible? She stopped when she saw lights on in her room. Callie was certain she hadn't left her light on and walked inside to find Lucas Jones stretched out on her bed with one of her mother's diaries in his hand. Had he read the one that said she was his daughter?

"What the hell are you doing here, Lucas and what are you doing with that?" Callie demanded.

"So, the bitch actually was carrying my child," Lucas snarled, "and she let that bastard Woods kill it."

The diary Lucas held was the one that told about her mother's rape one afternoon by Lucas and her subsequent discovery that she was pregnant by him and then her abortion of the child.

"Do you think she wanted to carry the child of rape?" Callie hissed. "Do you think she wanted to carry your child?" Callie shivered. She too was a child of rape—rape by the same man.

Lucas snorted. "I don't see why not. She carried my damned brother's children."

"Well, she loved him," Callie snapped.

"That whore only loved his money," Lucas snarled, "like any other damned whore."

Callie had heard enough and wanted to explode with anger at this horrible man who was her biological father. She suddenly remembered her mother's words written in the diary and she threw them back at Lucas without giving it any thought. "Well, considering your mother, Lucas, you'd certainly know a whore when you saw one."

Lucas's eyes went wide, and he jumped from the bed, tossing the diary aside. "What did you say?" he demanded with a fleeting look of confusion as he grabbed Callie's wrist. "I told you never to talk about my mama like that, Rachel." He slapped Callie and shook her hard. "Remember what you got the last time, whore?" he asked with a terrifying smile. "I think you enjoy getting punished with my cock, don't you, Rachel? My cock has got to be more enjoyable than that worthless brother's of mine." He ripped off her blouse and then her bra, staring at her breasts.

Callie screamed when his intentions finally dawned on her. This deranged asshole thought she was her mother and intended to rape her. Callie scooted up on the bed over the scattered diaries until her head pushed against the headboard. "Get out of my room, you son-of-a-bitch," Callie screamed and threw one of the diaries at him.

The little book hit Lucas in the face and seemed to bring him back to reality for a second. "Your mother aborted my child, bitch," he growled as he leaped atop Callie. "So, the way I see it, you owe me one in her place." His hand began to work at the button on her jeans. "If my seed took in her, I reckon it will take in you as well."

Callie screamed again as she scratched and fought the man atop her. "You can't do that," she yelled. "You can't make a baby with your own daughter, asshole. It would be a retard or something."

Something finally got through to the man and he stopped, staring down at Callie. "What the hell are you talking about, bitch?"

She reached for the oldest diary. "Read this one, asshole," Callie said, flinging the diary at Lucas. "I'm your fucking daughter."

Lucas took the book and began to read. "Well, I'll be damned," he said, glaring down at Callie. "I think my Rachel just got me this ranch after all."

Callie tried to roll away from the man, but he slapped her and pinned her to the bed again. "Daughter or no daughter," Lucas sneered, "I think I'll have a taste of that sweet spot between your legs anyhow. If you're mine, I can do with you as I please and I reckon I have a few years of catching up to do here."

Lucas began to chuckle. "It might even be more fun than holding William's head beneath the water in that cattle trough until the bubbles stopped coming up."

"What did you say?" Callie gasped. Her younger brother William Morgan Miller had drowned in a cattle trough on the ranch when he was seven and Callie was ten. He was buried in the family plot out back with her parents and grandparents and his death had been a bitter blow to them all. Was Lucas saying he was responsible?

"Did you think your sweet little brother ended up in that trough by accident?" he jeered. "It was a hot summer day and what boy doesn't want to go play in the water?" he laughed. "It was almost too easy to get rid of the little lord Miller." He reached for Callie again. "Now all I have to do is get rid of you, bitch, and this ranch will be mine by default."

As Lucas worked at getting her jeans open, Callie stretched her right arm over the edge of the bed and searched for the spot between the mattress and box springs where the handle of her mother's hunting knife protruded. When she found it, she let out a sigh of relief that Lucas took for something else.

"So, you want a little piece of daddy between your legs, huh, whore?" he asked with a demented chuckle. "Well, I intend to give it to you."

Callie was horrified at the thought and still reeled at his confession about her poor little brother, She clasped the handle of the hunting knife tight in her hand. As Lucas yanked her jeans down over her behind, Callie pulled the knife free and swung it blindly in Lucas's direction. She felt it connect and heard him scream as he jumped off her.

"I'll kill you for that bitch," he yelled and flung blood from the cut on his face in her direction.

Emboldened, Callie sprung to her knees and waved the knife. "Just try it, Daddy, and I'll slice your damned balls off and feed 'em to you." She could see his dark shape in the light coming from the hall. He held a hand to his face and Callie smiled to herself, hoping the cut went deep and would leave the bastard disfigured. "Get out of my house, Lucas," she screamed as loud as she could, hoping it would wake Rita in her room downstairs.

Lucas waved her mother's diary. "It won't be your house much longer, bitch. My lawyer is gonna have a field day with this little piece of work and you're gonna be out of MY house on your ass in no time at all." He laughed as he stuffed the diary into the front of his jeans, turned, and fled her room.

"And you're gonna be in jail for murdering my little brother," she yelled after him with tears of rage and reignited grief running down her face.

Callie tried to right herself to turn on the light and knocked the lamp off her bedside table. "Shit," she cursed and crawled off the bed to make her way to the wall switch to turn on the overhead light.

Outside, Mak tried to quiet his dog that tugged at the leash and had barked repeatedly at the house.

'Settle down, Pete, or I'm taking you back to the clinic and putting you in that crate you love so much," Mak said with a soft chuckle. He glanced up at the window when the light went out and then came back on a few minutes later. He turned to Rowdy who'd gotten out of his Jeep to join him and Pete on their walk. "I wonder what's going on with Callie," he said. "That light went on just after dark and has been on all evening. I was just walking over to see if she wanted to join this old reprobate and me on his walk."

Rowdy smiled as he studied the German Shepherd with a graying snout. Then he stopped to stare up at the window. "Is anyone else at home in there?"

Mak shrugged. "Sometimes Rita stays over," Mak said. "Why?"

"Because," Rowdy said, turning to trot toward the house, "when it got dark, Callie and I were sitting in Penny's Cafe in Miller's Crossing. Callie wasn't here to turn lights on in her room."

The sound of a pickup speeding away caught their attention as Pete barked again. "I think that was Lucas Jones's truck," Mak said, staring after the red taillights obscured by the white dust of the road.

"Oh, shit," Rowdy hissed and reached for the doorknob as a blood-curdling scream sounded from within the ranch house and Pete began to bark and scratch at the door.

Mak fumbled in his pocket. "I know, buddy, I'm going as fast as I can," he told the dog as he pulled a ring of keys out and sorted through them until he found the one he was looking for and opened the front door of the Miller Ranch house. "I've had this damned key on my ring for ten years, but I don't think I've ever used it until now," he told Rowdy.

He pushed the door open. The house was dark except for a light shining down from the upstairs hall and one glowing in the kitchen. They heard the sound of a woman weeping and hurried to the kitchen where they found Callie on her knees with Rita in her arms, sobbing. "Wake up, Rita. Please wake up."

Mak rushed to join her and pried her arms off the petite housekeeper so he could examine her. "Take her, please, Rowdy."

Rowdy took the sobbing Callie into his arms. He knew the older woman was dead. He'd seen his share of dead bodies in Afghanistan and always looked for the rising and falling of a chest when he came upon a prone figure like Rita. Her chest didn't move, and her skin was pale and waxy. Rowdy knew her heart had stopped pumping blood some time ago.

Callie wore a thin flannel robe and he could tell she wore nothing beneath it. "What the hell happened here, Cal?" he asked when he saw the fresh bruises on her face.

"Lucas," was all she said before dissolving into tears and burying her face into his shoulder.

Mak felt for a pulse in Rita's bruised neck before looking up at Rowdy with tears in his blue eyes and shaking his head to verify what Rowdy already knew. The old housekeeper was dead. Mak took out his phone and punched in a number. "This is Doctor Makenzie Woods at the Miller Ranch," he said in a professional tone, "and I'd like to report a murder." He was silent while the person on the other end spoke. "Please send the coroner and the sheriff to the main house. The housekeeper, Rita Torres has been killed."

Before the wailing of sirens broke the silence of the night on Miller Ranch, Zena and Cody Jackson rushed into the main house and the young, pregnant woman screamed when she saw her beloved aunt dead on the kitchen floor. "What happened to my Aunt Rita?" the girl sobbed as she stared at Mak for an answer.

"I'd say she was strangled," Mak said, pointing to Rita's eyes. "Those little pin-points of blood in her pupils tell me she was struggling for breath." He moved his hand and pointed at Rita's neck. "And these bruises were left by strong hands. Someone strangled the life out of poor Rita."

The corpulent sheriff came storming into the house then, followed by the coroner and some deputies. "What the hell is going on out here now, Woods?" he demanded, staring down at Rita's body.

"Someone murdered Rita Torres," Mak said in a tone that showed his lack of respect for the sheriff. "Strangled, I'd say," he said, turning his head to address the waiting coroner.

Zena sobbed into her husband's chest. "But who would want to kill my poor Aunt? Everybody loved her."

"Lucas Jones," Callie and Rowdy said in unison.

The sheriff's mouth fell open and his eyes narrowed. "Just because you have legal issues with Luke, Miss Miller, it gives you no right to accuse him with a heinous crime like murder."

Callie wiped her bruised eye and cleared her throat. "When I got home tonight," she told the scowling sheriff, "Lucas was in my room and he tried to rape me."

The sheriff gave a pig-like snort. "I hardly think Luke would have to rape the likes of you, Miss Miller."

Rowdy came to her defense, stepping between Callie and the offensive sheriff when he felt the woman's body stiffen in his arms. "And just what is that supposed to mean, you puffed up sack of lard?"

"It means," the sheriff said, pointing a stubby finger at Rowdy, "that everyone in Miller's Crossing knows this tramp will spread her legs for almost anybody to get what she wants."

Callie gasped and Rowdy's mouth fell open at the sheriff's foul words. "Why don't you ask her about her little tryst with that rich Arab in Afghanistan, soldier? She tried to tell everybody she'd been a hostage, but she came home with a filthy Arab brat in her belly and had to get rid of it." The sheriff chuckled. "She probably cut off her own damned hand just to get the sympathy from folks hereabouts."

Rowdy pointed at the fresh bruises on Callie's face. "And do you think she punched herself in the face?"

Callie pushed Rowdy aside to face the sheriff. "Lucas Jones was in my room when I got home," she snarled, "and he tried to rape me the same way he raped my mother all those years ago." She took a deep breath. "The bastard even admitted killing my little brother by drowning him in that cattle trough."

The sheriff snorted again. "That's a damned lie. Luke never killed anyone, and he certainly never had to rape Rachel, sweetheart. Everyone knows they were an item back in the day and I'd reckon you learned your whorin' ways from her. She threw my cousin over for your daddy, his money, and this damned ranch."

The sheriff watched as the coroner and his assistant lifted Rita's lifeless body onto a gurney. "I'll write in my report that poor Mrs. Torres likely interrupted a burglary and was killed by persons unknown at this time."

"You've got to be kidding," Rowdy gasped. "What about——"

"As for Miss Miller's bruised face, I'll write it up as merely rough sex also with persons unknown, whom she invited into her bed for consensual relations."

"Consensual?" Callie sputtered. "Well, when you find the bastard you can ask him how consensual it was when I sliced his face open with the hunting knife my mother kept hidden under the mattress."

The sheriff grinned. "I'll keep it in mind that you

admitted to assaulting your play partner with a deadly weapon, Miss Miller. You claim that partner was Luke, but I have no evidence he was anywhere near Miller Ranch tonight.

"Rowdy and I saw his truck speeding away from here just before we came in and found Callie with Rita," Mak said.

"And is this Rowdy fellow your latest conquest, peter-puffer?" the sheriff asked with a chuckle. "Maybe it was you and your faggot boyfriend who came in here and killed poor Rita and not Luke. I still have no proof he was even here on the ranch tonight other than the claims by a woman he's in litigation with and a couple of homos who depend on her for their lively hoods."

"Lucas Jones was here tonight," Zena said between sobs. "Tell him, Cody."

The new foreman glanced down at his wife and then at the sheriff. "She's right, Sheriff," Cody said hesitantly. "Lucas was here. He showed up at our door at about seven. Said he'd heard Miss Callie had given me his job and was fixin' up the carriage house for us to live in as the new foreman's residence."

"So," the sheriff said with a shrug, "Luke was here to congratulate a friend on his good fortune?"

"I'd hardly call it congratulations," Cody said, hugging his wife closer. "He told me that when he won his court case against Miss Callie and became the proper owner of Miller Ranch, he was going to dismiss me, run us out of the carriage house, and replace me with a true American who knew better than to marry up with a filthy redskin like Zena and pollute the white race by having a baby with her."

The sheriff chuckled. "Luke was never much of one for political correctness."

Zena turned to face the sheriff. "Lucas Jones was here tonight," she said, "and if Miss Callie says he assaulted her and killed my Aunt Rita, I believe her and will testify to it in court. Lucas didn't like Rita and she didn't like him. If she caught him in here sneaking around after Miss Callie fired him and told him to get the hell off Miller Ranch, then she likely threatened to call the police or something."

"As if the police in Miller's Crossing would have done a damned thing," Callie hissed, glaring at the sheriff.

"So, now we have a disgruntled Cheyenne squaw here to add to the accusations against Luke," the sheriff snorted. "I don't think anybody in the county will put much faith in any of it. Nobody's gonna believe a rich-bitch whore, a couple of her hired boys whom she's probably paying with the sweetmeat between her thighs, and the grieving Cheyenne niece of the murdered housekeeper of the same rich-bitch whore." He shook his head and his jowls shook. "No prosecutor in his right mind is gonna hang his hat on that." He motioned to his deputies. "Come on boys," he said, "let's get back to the office and maybe we can catch the last of the game."

The sheriff and his deputies left the house. "Is that really what stands for justice in Miller's Crossing?" Rowdy asked with a grunt. "I'd almost have thought I was back on the base in Mississippi."

"Some prejudices run nationwide," Mak said, "and there's nothing anybody can do about that."

Zena tugged at her husband's arm. "Let's go home, baby. I'm gonna have to call my cousins and give them the news about their mother and then start helping them to plan her funeral."

Callie stopped the young woman. "I want to help with anything I can, Zena. Have them take her body to Canton's. The family has an account there and," Callie's voice choked with a sob, "Rita was family. Get her the best and Miller Ranch will pay for everything. We can even bury her out back if they want."

Zena took Callie's hand. "Thank you, Miss Callie, but I'm sure my cousins will want to bury her beside their father in the cemetery on the reservation."

"Of course, they will," Callie said, suddenly embarrassed with her offer. "I'm sorry. I just wanted to keep her close to me." She broke down sobbing and Rowdy took her into his arms.

"Come on, sweetie," he whispered as Zena and Cody left along with Mak and his dog Pete, "let's get you upstairs and into your bed for some much-needed rest."

She looked up at him with her red, tear-stained eyes wide. "What if Lucas comes back? I think he must still have a key to the house."

Rowdy hugged the trembling woman close. "Don't worry, Cal," he said and kissed the top of her head, "I'll sit up here with you and keep you safe from that bastard while you sleep."

❧ 13 ❧

Callie was at the stock tanks again with Rita tugging her arm after they saw William's clothes folded on the ground with his straw cowboy hat resting atop them and his dirty boots. When William didn't show up for supper, when Rita was making his favorite crunchy tacos, her father had organized a search for his son. She and Rita had walked down to the cattle tanks, calling his name though Callie knew her brother wouldn't come to the tanks for a swim after their father had tanned their behinds last summer for sneaking off together, but Callie still screamed when she saw the pale body, floating face down in the water, wearing his favorite super-hero underpants. Rita had screamed William's name and jumped into the water, but it was too late. William Miller was dead, and Callie had cried.

Callie woke with tears on her face in Rowdy's arms.

"You were having a bad dream," he said, rubbing her hair, "You kept calling out a name. Who is William?"

"My little brother," Callie said, weeping in Rowdy's arms. "He drowned in the cattle tanks south of the barn and last night Lucas told me he was the one who did it." She wept and

Rowdy held her. He didn't speak, he just held her and let her cry until she couldn't cry anymore.

Callie's head throbbed behind her eyes from crying. What was she going to do without Rita? Zena had been working with her aunt at the ranch for three years now, but was she ready to take on all that responsibility with the baby coming in a few months?

Rita had been doing the cooking and cleaning in the big house for almost twenty-five years. She had known all the Miller family secrets and Callie wished she'd sat down with the woman and picked her brain. Why was hindsight always so much better than foresight?

Rita's graveside services were held on the Cheyenne Reservation where she and her children lived and conducted by a Cheyenne shaman rather than a Christian minister. Rita had been a casual churchgoer, but her daughter Marta had reverted to the old Cheyenne faith some years earlier in an effort to connect with her native roots like so many of the younger generation on the Reservation. A Christian minister had officiated at the service held at the funeral home, which had been filled to capacity with friends and mourners. Zena had been correct, everyone who knew Rita Torrez had loved her.

Callie cooked Sunday Supper that week in honor of Rita. She made Rita's favorite fried chicken with mashed potatoes, sweet corn, white cream gravy, and big, fluffy biscuits. Zena helped her and they made several apple pies the way Rita had taught them to serve for desert.

"What are they doing to hunt down that son-of-a-bitch who killed her?" George Jr., Rita's son, asked as he served himself a second helping of pie.

Zena snorted in a fair mimic of her aunt. "That bastard sheriff ain't gonna do a damned thing," she said and sipped her coffee. "He won't even admit to the possibility that his cousin was here that night even though there were eye-witnesses to the fact. I fear there'll be no white man's justice for poor Aunt Rita."

George Jr. took out his hunting knife and tossed it into the air. "Perhaps it's time for some Cheyenne justice then."

Callie grinned. "I used a knife almost just like that one to slice his damned face open," she said, "but I have no problem with you taking his damned scalp if you can find him. I bet Rita would appreciate it decorating her pretty pink granite tombstone."

Zena nodded with a grin on her pretty face. "It might even ease uncle George's spirit some that he rests beneath a girlie pink marker if Lucas Jones's scalp hung on that stone."

"I think we should stake him out naked by a damned red ant hill," Cody said, "and then you can take his scalp after the ants have done their business."

Rowdy grinned. "Zena, I think you've turned this skinny white boy into a savage to be proud of."

Zena shook her head as she put the final bite of pie into her mouth. "He reads too many Western novels," she said. "The Cheyenne never staked white men over anthills. That was the Comanche down in Texas."

Rowdy shrugged his broad shoulders. "Cheyenne or Comanche," he said, "justice is justice and I'm fine with it any way it comes. Lucas Jones is a rapist and murderer of women and children. He deserves to be punished."

Zena smiled. "I knew there was a reason my aunt liked you, Mr. Rowdy."

"You mean besides tomatoes, sweet corn, and fresh eggs?"

"Besides all that," Zena said. "Aunt Rita said you had the soul of a warrior and would look out for Miss Callie and the rest of us like one of the Dog Soldiers the old men talk about around the campfires."

Rowdy's face fell. "I didn't do a very good job of looking out for Miss Rita though, did I?"

Marta, Rita's daughter, who'd been silent up until now

stood and spoke with dignity and authority, wearing fringed white doeskin decorated with colorful trade beads. "The spirits tell me that you will avenge my mother, Mr. Waters, and prove her faith in you as a warrior soul." She picked up her half-eaten plate and carried it across the patio and into the kitchen.

George Jr. stood as well. "If my sister has seen you avenging our mother, Mr. Waters, then avenged she will be and I'm content with that however it might come to pass," he said and followed his sister into the house.

"Wow," Rowdy said, releasing the breath he'd been holding, "talk about performance anxiety."

Callie patted his hand and kissed his cheek. "I'm sure you'll do fine, Mr., Waters," she said with a grin, "and tomorrow we'll ride up on the mesa and I'll show you where there are a couple of really big red anthills."

Everyone laughed, but Rowdy felt uneasy. Would Rita's spirit be unable to rest if he didn't mete out justice for her? Should he have sought justice for his men in Afghanistan and helped to ferret out Al Asadi and bomb his encampment with that drone? Afghani native people, like the native Americans around this table, believed in getting justice for the lost souls of their people. Was it time for him to give up the Christian religion of his Mama back in Missouri and take up the native beliefs of the people here in Montana? He thought about the little housekeeper wrapping her arms around him and thanking him for the fresh produce and thought maybe it was.

"Your meal was really good, Callie," Rowdy said as he helped to dry and put away the dishes after everyone had gone.

"Thanks," she said. "It was Rita's favorite and I cooked it for her every month or so to give her a break from the kitchen." Callie smiled. "She loved Kentucky Fried Chicken but didn't like the brown gravy they serve with it, so I always made her the white cream gravy." Her voice broke with sobs and Rowdy rushed to her and took her into his arms while she grieved.

"You really loved that old woman, didn't you?" he asked, whispering into her bright red hair as he held her.

"She's been with me since I was a girl," Callie replied, "and like a second mother to me."

"I'm so sorry you've had to go through all of this, but it will get better soon."

Callie pulled away. "I don't see how with Lucas still out there."

"And with his court case hanging over your head?" Rowdy took a deep breath. "I think I know why you're so worried about that. I read some of your mama's diaries while you were asleep."

Callie stared up at the man. "Then you know he's my real father and not Morgan Miller?" She dashed the tears from her face in anger and embarrassment. How dare he read those personal diaries. He was no better than Lucas. "I'm just the bastard child of a bastard, and no more entitled to this ranch than he is." Callie tossed the dish towel onto the counter. "You probably think I'm a deceitful fraud just like my mother was." She began to sob again. "I'm just a dirty bastard and don't deserve to be living in this Miller house or carry the Miller name. I'm not a Miller any more than Lucas is and when he takes that before a judge, I'll be tossed out of here on my ass. I'm just the illegitimate child of rape my mother pawned off on another man as his."

"I'm illegitimate," Rowdy said with a sigh as he touched her shoulder.

"What?" Callie gasped, jerking her head up to stare into his soft brown eyes.

"I'm illegitimate too. My mother wasn't married to my father and that bastard ran off and left her when she told him he'd knocked her up."

"But at least she told him," Callie said. "My mother didn't

tell Lucas she was pregnant. Instead, she hid it from him and tricked another man into marrying her." Callie dropped into one of the chairs at the table. "My life is a damned lie," she sobbed. "I'm a damned lie."

Rowdy narrowed his eyes as he studied the weeping woman. "Did you read all your mother's diaries?"

Callie shook her head. "All but the last two, I think."

"Wait here," Rowdy said and rushed from the room.

He returned with one of her mother's diaries open in his hand. "Read this," he said, handing her the book.

Callie took the diary and noted the date of the entry. It was just after she'd joined MET and left for Afghanistan.

"I told Morgan the truth today. I didn't know what to expect but he was talking about going into Missoula to rewrite our wills, so I thought it was time. The man never ceases to amaze me. He said Callie had been his daughter for over thirty years and as far as he was concerned, she'd be his daughter for the rest of his life no matter how she'd been conceived. Lucas might have been the one to plant the seed, but he'd been the one who cared for the plant. Callista Jane Miller was his daughter and heir to Miller Ranch the way he'd raised her to be. He may be a fuck around asshole like his daddy was, but I love that damned man."

Callie lifted her head to stare at Rowdy with her mouth open in surprise. "He may not have been your sperm donor, Callie, but Morgan Miller was your father and he loved you."

"And my real father just wanted to have sex with me," she said in disgust. "What kind of man does that?"

"No man at all in my way of thinking," Rowdy said. "Morgan Miller was a true man," he said, "and one you should be proud to call your real father."

Callie could see her father's face as plain before her as if he were standing there. She remembered his arms around her when she left for Afghanistan and tears rolled down her face. "He knew my mother's secret and he loved me anyhow?"

"You were born his baby, Callie," Rowdy said, holding her

close, "and he loved you the way any man would love his child."

"But I wasn't his child," Callie wept into his shoulder. "I'm Lucas Jones's child and my mother lied about it all."

"Morgan Miller didn't care about that, Callie, and he left you this ranch in his will, knowing the truth. You are Callista Jane Miller and the rightful owner of Miller Ranch," Rowdy told her and the force with which he said the words made her believe it.

Callie clutched the diary in her hand. "If Lucas is going to use one of my mother's diaries against me in court to try and get this ranch," she said with fire in her green eyes, "then I can do the same to prove daddy knew about the circumstances of my birth and left me the ranch anyway."

Rowdy hugged her close. "That's my girl," he said with a broad smile. "That bastard isn't gonna know what hit him."

Callie yawned. "I suppose this means I'm gonna need to make a trip into Missoula tomorrow to chat with my attorney." She kissed his cheek. "What do you have on your plate for tomorrow?"

Rowdy grinned. "First, I need to drive up to the cabin to check on things there and give Princess a little attention, then it's back to painting in the carriage house," Rowdy said, rolling his eyes. "I swear that woman changes her mind twice a day about which color is supposed to go in which room."

"Do you want me to talk to her?" Callie offered. "Are all the cabinets finished?"

"Oh, yah," he said, "Cody and I had those knocked out in a couple of days and he even built a linen closet in the bathroom on his own."

Callie smiled. "I'm glad you and Cody are getting on well."

"I don't know why we wouldn't. He likes to tinker around with things as much as I do to try and make something useful out of what others might think of as junk."

"Like a hundred-year-old carriage house that's seen better days?"

"And a hundred-fifty-year-old cabin," Callie said with a grin. "What else do you have planned for up there?"

"Besides filling my freezer, pantry, and woodshed for the winter?" he said. "Not too much. I need to finish shingling the barn so poor Princess has a dry place for the winter, but then it's just gonna be prepping food so I don't starve, and splitting wood, so I don't freeze."

Callie nodded. "A soul could get stuck up there for weeks with that terrible road if there was a big snow."

"Maybe I should think about buying a horse," he said with a grin. "It could keep Princess company and be my means to get down the mountain should things get nasty up there."

"Do you know about the old back trail that runs down from there to the ranch?"

Rowdy furrowed his brow in thought. "You mean that washed out old path behind the barn?"

"That would be the one," Callie said. "I used to hike it up to the cabin when I was a kid and grandma was up there to get away from grandpa and his shenanigans." She kissed his cheek again. "You might wanna hike it all the way down and scope out deadfall for your wood collection."

Rowdy stood, confident Callie was in a better mood. "Well, I guess I'll call it a night and get out of your hair early in the morning." He kissed her cheek and went up the stairs to the guest room he'd been using while working on the carriage house.

Callie watched him go and then ran her hand over the leather cover of her mother's diary. "I'm glad you told him, Mama," Callie whispered to the book. "I'm glad you didn't go to the grave with that secret on your soul and I'm glad he went to his grave knowing the truth."

❧ 14 ❧

As Rowdy neared the cabin, his phone rang. He let it go to voicemail because he didn't like to drive the steep, narrow road with the phone in his hand. He'd check the message when he got to the cabin and took care of Princess. He smiled to himself, thinking his men would have found it amusing that their tough sergeant would be taking care of a calf and let it wrap itself around his heart the way Princess had.

He also wondered what they'd think about the pretty redhead who'd done much the same thing. She was a wildcat in the sack and fulfilled his needs sexually like no woman Rowdy had ever known, but she was also vulnerable and made him want to protect her. Had that been Rita's doing? Had the old Cheyenne woman put some sort of native glamor upon him where Callie Miller was concerned? He shook his head as he parked the Jeep and got out. No, it was all about the little head between his legs. He wanted to protect Callie because he wanted to spend more time in bed with her.

As soon as Rowdy left the jeep, the calf began bawling at the fence. "Alright, Princess, I'm coming," he said with a chuckle. By the time he got there, the rambunctious calf had mounted the fence and almost over it to meet him. Rowdy reached into his pocket for her dried apple treat but came out empty. "I gotta go to the house for your treat, girl. Wanna come along with me?"

The calf clattered over the fence, ran to his side, and began to nudge at Rowdy's pocket. "I told you we had to go to the house to get more," he said as he petted the spot on her head between her ears. Princess pressed close into him as they climbed the step onto the porch, and he opened the cabin door.

Rowdy breathed in the smells of home. The scent of wood smoke and ashes from the fireplace hung in the cool dry air and, he thought, the lingering aroma of Callie and the amazing sex they'd had here before going down to the ranch. As nice as the ranch house was down below, Rowdy thought he preferred the simple cabin and the simpler life up here on the mountain.

Princess, who'd followed him inside, nudged his pocket again and Rowdy went to the clear glass canister on the counter to pull out a handful of treats to shove into his pocket. He offered one to Princess who took it greedily and began to chew. Knowing she needed more than the slices of dried apple in her diet, Rowdy prepared a bottle, took a seat on the couch, and began to feed his hungry charge.

As he sat, relaxing while the calf fed, Rowdy pulled out his phone and found his voicemail. "Hey, Sarge, this is Billy, Billy Dane, and I think I'm in trouble here." There was a long pause before Billy spoke again and Rowdy was fearful the young man was in some sort of imminent peril before he spoke again. "Remember that job I called you about? Well, it's moving cattle like I said, but I think these guys are stealing them off the ranches." Billy went silent again. "If you don't hear from me again, Sarge, it's because Free Wheelin's done away with me. We're off to pick up Bar-M cattle on some ranch to hell and gone from Missoula. We was always told to cull Bar-M cattle from our hauls before, but now the boss says their fair game for the takin'. I'm worried I've gotten myself into something I'm not gonna be able to get myself out of, Sarge."

The call ended and Princess spit out the red rubber nipple of the empty bottle. Rowdy got up and began to pace. He shooed the calf outside to do her business and closed the door. He studied the old brand burned into the door frame—Bar-M —the Miller Ranch brand for their cattle and horses. "Damnit, Billy, what sorta shit have you gone and gotten yourself into now?" Rowdy said into the empty room.

Rowdy picked up his phone and started to punch in Callie's number but remembered she was driving into Missoula to see her attorney and punched in Cody's instead.

"Yah?" Cody answered. "I'm kinda busy here, so make it short and sweet."

"Sorry to bother you on a workday, Cody, but this is Rowdy, and I just came into some information regarding Miller Ranch and her cattle I thought you should hear."

"What about the ranch's cattle?" Cody asked, giving Rowdy his full attention now.

"Well, I have a buddy I served with in Afghanistan, and he just called me to say that this outfit he signed on with called Free Wheeling might be into stealing cattle off ranches and that they'd just been ordered to pick up cattle with the Bar-M brand out here."

"Damnit," Cody cursed, "I had a feelin' those trucks runnin' out here were up to no good."

"I was gonna call Callie," Rowdy said, "but I think she was going to see her lawyer today about Lucas's lawsuit."

"Yah, she let out of here pretty early, but then so did you," he added with a chuckle. "The boss kick you out of bed early today?"

Rowdy frowned. He didn't know how he felt about the whole ranch knowing he and Callie shared a bed from time to time. "I slept in my own room last night, smart ass. I had to get up early to drive up the mountain and see to Princess before driving back down to fight with your pregnant wife about what paint goes where today."

Cody laughed. "You should try settling what we're gonna have for supper every night."

"Why do you think I live up here on the mountain with a cow and not a woman?"

Cody continued to laugh. "Ok, what's this critical news you have for me about Miller Ranch cattle, buddy, so I can get back to work."

"Bar-M is the Miller brand, isn't it?" Rowdy asked to head the conversation in the right direction.

"Sure is, and we'll probably start branding the new calves in a week or two which is why I need to get this shit all taken care of around here before we head out to the range."

"So, my buddy was just ordered to start picking up Miller Ranch cattle, loading them into those Free Wheeling trucks, and hauling them off to Missoula." Rowdy took a breath. "What do you think we should do about it?"

Cody was silent on the other end. "I don't think you should do a damned thing, buddy, but if the boys and me can track down where the trucks are, we'll ride in and give 'em the surprise of their lives."

"My friend said they were headed this way from Missoula now," Rowdy said, "and I can act as a lookout from up here at the cabin and let you know where I see the truck or trucks."

"That would be a real help, man," Cody said with a sigh. "In the meantime, I'll call the sheriff and give him a heads up on the situation."

Rowdy snorted. "Do you really think that fat lard ass is gonna do anything for Callie and her ranch?"

"You're probably right. I'll put a call into the cattle board as well. They have guys paid to do nothing but investigate rustling claims."

"I can't believe we're talking about cattle rustlers in this day and age," Rowdy said with a soft chuckle. "It's more like something out of Rawhide or The Virginian."

"It's more common than you'd think and if these Free Wheeling trucks are behind it, it's been hitting ranchers around here pretty hard." Cody coughed. "I think I'd better make a few more calls while I'm at it. Get on back down here to the ranch and I'll explain to Zena why you won't be there to paint today."

Rowdy smiled. Chasing modern cattle rustlers wasn't what he had in mind for his day, but he thought it might be preferable to spending it arguing with the pregnant Mrs. Jackson. He made certain Princess was back and secure in her pen and went through the garden to collect the ripest produce before watering and feeding his chickens and collecting the eggs. He'd bring all of it to the ranch and would leave it with Zena in the kitchen. Perhaps some of it would end up on his plate for supper tonight.

Rowdy found his phone and punched in Billy Dane's number. Maybe he could get a location from the young man and not have to wait on the roof, looking for trucks.

"Hey, Sarge, thanks for callin' me back," Billy said, and Rowdy could tell from the tone of his voice that he probably couldn't talk.

"You have time to chat now or should I touch back with you later?"

"Workin' right now, Sarge, but maybe when I get back from this Mason's Wells place, we can talk. How's your PT goin'? Been up to the VA in Missoula to see that new doc Bragg set you up with?"

"Not yet, Billy. I think my appointment is for next Wednesday at one-thirty."

"Well, maybe we can catch lunch then, Sarge. Gotta go. Talk at ya later."

"Mason's Wells?" Rowdy added, hoping to get a confirmation from the young man before he hung up.

"Yep," he said with a forced chuckle. "Bye, Sarge." Billy hung up and Rowdy started the old Cherokee.

He hurried down the mountain road faster than he generally drove it, but he knew this information would be important to Cody and the other cowboys. Rowdy had no idea what they had in mind, but he was glad he carried his old service pistol in the rear of the Jeep. In the old westerns, the posse would ride up on the offending rustlers, there'd be a shootout, and the rustlers would always lose. He hoped that would be the case today, but he had no way of knowing.

He looked up at the pristine blue sky and smiled where a few fluffy white clouds hung above the towering mountains in the distance. At least it was a beautiful day for a shootout if they had to have one. Rowdy parked on the drive beside an unfamiliar pick up with Littleton Ranch stenciled on the door, gathered the produce from the back of his vehicle and went inside.

"You have more yummy things for us, Mr. Rowdy?" Zena said without looking him in the eyes and Rowdy got the feeling the new head housekeeper wasn't happy about having the painting delayed in her residence.

"I had to pick it, or it was gonna spoil in the garden," he said, "and I brought eggs since they're beginning to pile up there without me to eat a few every day."

"Well, they'll get eaten here," she said with a grin that eased the tension. "I'll have Cody take some down to the bunkhouse along with some of these beautiful tomatoes. The boys down there will polish 'em off in no time."

"Is Cody here?" he asked. "I have some information to relay about that truck coming in from Missoula."

"They're all in the den cleaning their guns," Zena said with a frown. "I don't like them going out there all hopped up like this with loaded guns."

Rowdy turned toward the den. "Gotta be ready for bear, Mrs. Jackson. There's no tellin' what they're gonna come at us with."

Zena shook her head as she sorted through the produce. "You men are all alike," she muttered, "but if you come back here with my Cody all shot up, there'll be hell to pay."

Rowdy smiled to himself, knowing the young Cheyenne woman meant every word and would certainly make life miserable for everyone if they brought Cody home injured. When he walked into the smoky den, everyone looked up. "Well, it's about damned time," Cody said in a teasing tone. "Princess have you occupied up there?"

"She wasn't happy to see me go, that's for certain."

"Spoiled females are spoiled females, no matter the species," an unfamiliar man sitting beside Cody said as the other men laughed in agreement.

This is the fella I was telling you about, Luther, Rowdy Waters. He's been doing the fixin' on the carriage house Zena and I are living in now."

The gray-headed man in his late fifties or early sixties extended his tanned and wrinkled hand. "You do nice work, son. I'm real impressed with those cabinets."

Rowdy felt his cheeks begin to burn with embarrassment as he took the good-natured man's hand. "Thank you, sir, but Cody did most of the work. I just gave him the simple directions and he followed the plan to a T."

"But they were your idea and your plan, son." He leaned in close to Rowdy and grinned. "Don't never brush off a man's compliment on your work, boy. You never know when he might be of a mind to hire ya for some work of his own that needs doin'."

Rowdy stepped back in surprise. "Oh, I don't know, Sir," he said with a glance at the sour face Zena wore as she refilled coffee cups, "I'm pretty much covered up with work here then

I've got to get back up the mountain and get the cabin ready for winter before the first snow flies."

"Got me a cabin up on Bald mountain," he said with a glance at Zena, "and the wife's been after me for cabinets in it for decades now. I thought they might be a nice surprise for her birthday in mid-September," he said with a hopeful grin on his weathered face. "I'd be willin' to pay ya right good. I'm Luther Littleton from Littleton Ranch up the road from here a piece." He nodded to the west. "Cody says you might have a line on those thievin' rustlers who've been workin' the herds hereabouts." The old man scratched his thinning gray hair. "I've lost over a hundred head to those bastards over the last three months. They never hit in the same place twice. It's as if they know exactly where the most prime bulls and cows are being kept."

Rowdy's eyes scanned the room. Could one of these men be working along with Lucas?

"I do, as a matter of fact," Rowdy said as all the eyes in the room focused on him. "Do y'all know where Mason's Wells is located?"

"Sure do," one of the younger hands offered, "It's where the bulk of our herd is settled for the time being. Why?"

"Because, according to my friend, Billy, it's where the rustlers are on their way to hit now."

"Oh, dear God," Cody yelped as he jumped to his feet, "why didn't you say that right off?" He too scanned the room. "Hitch up, boys," he said in a firm voice, "we can be there in fifteen minutes if we ride hard."

"We're riding there on horseback?" Rowdy gasped.

"You can ride with me and Luther here in the air-conditioned Ford." He chuckled as he started the engine. We old men and wussies have to stick together after all."

"Hold it a minute," Rowdy said and jumped out of the truck. He hurried to the jeep, opened the back, and rummaged around until he found what he was looking for.

When he returned, he carried a Glock 17 and two extra clips. He checked the weapon and put the clips in a vest pocket. "Now I'm ready to rock and roll."

"I like this one, Cody," Luther said with a broad smile. "Miss Callie's gonna be lucky if I don't steal this one away from her."

"I think Miss Callie has something to offer him you can't come close to matching," Cody replied with a wink at Rowdy.

"Could be," Luther said," but that don't mean I ain't gonna try."

Cody grinned and winked at Rowdy. "You can try, Luther. You can try."

🏵 15 🏵

Callie sat on edge in her lawyer's office, waiting for him to finish with another client. What was she even doing here? She should be back on the ranch tending to ranch business. What was she thinking? This firm had handled Miller Ranch business for almost a century. Howard Carlisle knew all the Miller's dirty little secrets. He probably already knew about the circumstances of her birth. Why had she thought it so important to put this on the very top of her to-do list for today?

"Mr. Carlisle is ready for you now, Miss Miller," the pretty receptionist said and beckoned Callie toward the lawyer's office. "But please keep it brief if you can, Miss. We fit you in because your family is a long-time client, but we're really backed up today."

"I'll keep that in mind," Callie said as the girl opened Mr. Carlisle's office door.

Callie took a seat in the plush Queen Anne chair across from Mr. Carlisle's ornately carved desk. "What can I do for you today, Miss Miller?" the tall, pale lawyer with a receding hairline asked.

"It's about this lawsuit with Lucas Jones," Callie said.

Carlisle rolled his eyes. "The man's got tenacity, I'll give him that. He's filed a number of these frivolous suits over the years, Miss Miller, but the judges have tossed them all." He sipped his coffee. "Is there a reason you think this one has more merit than any of the others?"

"You know then, that he's the illegitimate son of my grandfather?"

Carlisle opened a folder and ran his finger down the page. "His mother is a strumpet," he said with a sigh without looking up from the page, "One Doris Jones who resides in Miller's Crossing in a lovely little bungalow purchased for her and her son by your grandfather Morgan Miller Sr Is there anything else on your mind today?"

Callie took a deep breath in order to compose herself for the embarrassing question she had to ask. "And were you aware that I'm, in reality, the illegitimate daughter of Lucas Jones, put into my mother's womb by rape?" She batted back tears of shame and rage at the man.

Carlisle handed her a tissue. Those things must be a huge part of his office budget every year. "As a matter of fact," Mr. Carlisle said as he returned to his oxblood red leather chair and sat, "your parents came in here to relate that fact to me shortly before their terrible accident."

"And my father, hmm, well, Morgan Miller Jr. who'd thought me his daughter for all those years, didn't balk at my mother's deception and denounce me as the owner and manager of Miller Ranch?"

Mr. Carlisle smiled a warm, heartfelt smile. "On the contrary, Miss Miller, he said, "Morgan couldn't have been more pleased. We redrafted both their wills and your father was adamant that you be named owner and operator of Miller Ranch in the event of both he and your mother's death." Now was there anything else I can assist you with today?"

Callie dug into her purse and brought out her mother's

diary from back at that time. She'd marked the page and opened it. "This is my mother's diary that tells about her telling my father the truth and his reaction. I thought you might want to use it after Lucas uses another one of Mama's diaries to denounce me as a bastard and a fraud when it comes to the ownership of Miller Ranch," she said with a deep sigh.

"It was very fortuitous for you that you found that entry because I was wondering how we were going to counter his attorney's claims of fraud on your behalf."

Callie's eyes went wide. "I never knew until I began reading Mama's diaries. I've always thought Morgan Miller was my father and had no reason to think otherwise."

Carlisle nodded with a soft smile on his face. "I like the way that sounds coming from you, Miss Miller."

Callie's face twisted in confusion and the attorney smiled. "I'd like you to memorize those words and repeat them on the stand anytime you are asked about what you knew about your parentage and when you learned the truth." He scribbled something on a note pad, tore the paper off, and handed it to Callie. It read: I've always thought Morgan Miller was my daddy and had no reason to think otherwise until I found my mama's diaries. Callie stared across the desk at Carlisle. "Do you think my parroting this will make a difference?"

"Along with everything else I intend to present and Lucas Jones's general surly attitude, I think it should do the trick." He gave Callie a reassuring smile. "Remember, I've been in the courtroom with Mr. Jones on this matter before and he generally puts his big foot in his mouth at some point and pisses off the judge enough to get everything thrown out— along with himself." Carlisle chuckled. "I'm surprised he can even find an attorney in this county to take the case anymore." The attorney stood and offered his hand, signaling to Callie their meeting was at an end and she should go.

Callie stood and took his hand. "Thank you, Mr. Carlisle. I hope you're right about this."

"Just go on home to your ranch, Miss Miller, and don't give any of this another thought. Lucas Jones has no legal standing here and he never has."

☙❧

Rowdy drove in his Jeep Cherokee behind Cody on the dusty ranch road toward Mason's Wells where stock tanks stood for the thirsty cattle. Cody told him three different ranches shared the tanks and it would be the perfect place for rustlers to load cattle with a variety of brands.

Luther had called some additional ranchers who'd lost cattle over the past year, explaining what they'd learned from Rowdy about the Free Wheeling operation and their caravan out to Mason's Wells had expanded to a dozen ranch vehicle filled with angry, armed men. Cody had called Sheriff Harris who'd all but blown him off until Luther got on the phone and mentioned his large contributions to Harris's campaign for re-election. The sheriff's car led the group and two deputy vehicles made up the rear.

The walkie-talkie on the seat crackled and the sheriff's voice boomed into the quiet. "I see the truck up ahead, backing up to the cattle chute. Looks like we're gonna get 'em before they actually take possession of any cattle. Let's stop here and give 'em time to load up some cattle, so we have something to actually charge the sons-of-bitches with."

The vehicles slowed on the gravel road until they all came to a halt in sight of the tanks and the windmill pumping up the water to fill them. Rowdy was watching the big blades of the mill spin when he caught sight of something and yelled, "Get down! Sniper in the windmill."

Bullets began to ping off the hoods of the trucks and Rowdy cursed when one shattered his windshield. "Return fire," the sergeant in him yelled as his military training took over by instinct.

The sound of gunfire echoed across the grassland in the canyon where the wells were located, scattering the cattle that had come to the stock tanks. Rowdy frowned as cattle raced past the vehicles. Well, there goes our evidence of rustling.

Rowdy worked his way forward to the sheriff's car, where a bullet or bullets had taken out the light bar across the top of the squad car. He took the walkie from the sheriff's trembling hand and spoke into it with authority. "Move forward, arms at the ready, but keep low and to the bushes, so they don't have a shot. When we're close enough," Rowdy said, "I'll take out their sniper in the windmill."

"You some kind of soldier or something?" the sheriff asked Rowdy with his eyes wide.

"Or something," Rowdy said as he returned the walkie to the man. "You have my six?" he asked the trembling lawman as he moved past him with his Glock in hand. "How much ammo you have with you for that rifle in the back window or is that just for show?"

The sheriff coughed to clear his throat. "It's loaded with five in the tube and one in the pipe, but I'm not sure if there are any more rounds in a box in the trunk," he said with a shrug of his uniform-clad shoulder. "Never had much cause to check it before."

Rowdy rolled his eyes, wondering how this worthless shit ever got elected to this position if he didn't even know firearms. He reached for the door handle as a round pinged off the roof above his head. The sniper was watching the sheriff's vehicle, wrongly figuring the man would be heading up the invasion force.

Rowdy waited a few minutes and then opened the door, crawled into the back seat, and grabbed the rifle from the rack as more bullets pinged off the roof of the squad car.

"Damn, that guy is persistent," Rowdy growled when he slid out of the car and back into the weeds.

"Think you can knock him down from here?" the sheriff asked as Rowdy lined up the shot without benefit of a scope.

"I can try," Rowdy said and pulled the trigger. The cowboys in the trucks behind them cheered when they saw the man fall from the windmill. "Let's move out," he said into the radio, "but stay low and keep to the brush for concealment as much as you can. I hate making notifications to next of kin."

Cody joined Rowdy at the sheriff's car and slapped his back. "That was a great shot, man. I had no idea you were a crack shot along with being a great carpenter."

Rowdy shrugged. "My grandpa and mama took me hunting as a kid," he said. "It was learn to shoot or go without meat in the freezer for the winter." He took a deep breath and glanced at the stock tanks. "The army just honed the skills a little, I guess."

Cody chuckled. "Honed it razor-sharp, I'd say."

"Let's move out and get this over with," Rowdy said as others joined them at the sheriff's car.

He motioned for half the men to cross the road and move toward the tanks in the bushes there while he, the sheriff, and a few others crept up on the rustlers from their side. When they came close to the tanks and saw that the men were busy loading the cattle into the truck, the sheriff regained his courage and stood with his pistol drawn. "You boys can just stop what you're doing now," he yelled, "and put your thieving hands up."

The men stopped and turned to face a dozen men with guns in their hands. One of them stepped forward. "I don't know what you mean by that, sheriff," he said, raising his hands, "we're here to pick up cattle for transport that were contracted to Free Wheeling by the owner."

The sheriff turned to Cody. "Is that true, Mr. Jackson? Did

your boss Miss Miller sell cattle and arrange their transport with this Free Wheeling outfit?"

"Not to my knowledge, Sheriff," Cody said, "and as I'm her foreman, I think she'd have told me about cattle being moved off the ranch."

"I'm sure she would have," the sheriff said as he pointed his service weapon at the lead rustler. "Let's take these men into custody," he yelled to his deputies.

Everyone stopped when a man staggered out of the brush from beneath the windmill with a bloody shoulder.

"Billy?" Rowdy gasped and ran to catch the young man before he fell. "Was that you up there shooting at us, Billy?"

"Kirkman there told me to hold you off while they loaded the cattle," Billy Dane said to Rowdy as the sheriff and Luther joined them.

"That Kirkman there?" the sheriff asked, nodding at the man who'd stepped forward. "He the boss of this operation?"

"He's the on-sight supervisor," Billy said with a groan, "but Mr. Wheeler back in Missoula is the big boss who tells us which ranches to pick cattle up at."

"Shut your big mouth, Dane," Kirkman yelled.

The sheriff pressed closer to Billy. "And just how does this Wheeler all the way over in Missoula get his information about which ranches to hit out here?" he asked with a smug smile.

"Jones," Billy moaned as Rowdy eased the young man to the ground. "Lucas Jones feeds him the information. "He's some sorta ranch foreman out here and knows all the other ranch foremen who tell him where the herds will be."

"Lucas fucking Jones is behind this?" Rowdy growled at the sheriff, who stood staring down at Billy Dane with his mouth open.

The sheriff kicked Billy's leg hard. "This man's a thief and obviously a liar trying to set Luke up to take the fall for someone else's misdeeds." His eyes shot to Cody and then to

Luther, who stood beside the other ranch owners. "Likely another ranch foreman with money to gain in dealing with this Wheeler fellow in Missoula and not Luke."

Billy tugged on Rowdy's arm. "It's Lucas Jones who is Wheeler's contact out here on the ranches, Sarge and it's Wheeler who gives Kirkman the orders about where to pick up the cattle."

A shot rang out and Billy's head jerked back as a bullet from Kirkman's pistol pierced his skull. More shots were fired by the sheriff and his deputies, sending Kirkman to the ground dead.

"Billy," Rowdy screamed and hugged the bloody head of the young private to his chest as tears ran down his face.

"And just what was your involvement in all of this, Mr. Waters?" the sheriff sneered. "I'd almost wager you were this Wheeler fellows connection here on the ground and not poor Luke, who you've had it in for since day one. We all know you've been diddling that little one-handed tramp on Miller Ranch." He glanced at the ranch owners with Luther who whispered together and nodded. "She's likely where you've been getting your information to pass on to that big shot in Missoula. You've been fucking her and then using the information she gives you to fuck over the other hard-working ranchers in my county."

"That's a damned lie," Cody shouted. "Neither Rowdy nor Miss Callie would have anything to do with stealing cattle from other ranches, but Lucas is certainly the sorta man who would."

"Luke swears this ranch is his," the sheriff countered, "so why would he have these thieves steal cattle he sees as his?"

Rowdy eased Billy's body back to the ground and stood. "That boy told me they'd been told not to take Bar-M cattle before," he said to Luther and the other ranchers, "and then recently they'd been told Bar-M beef was now fair game and that's why the truck was out here today. They were here to collect Bar-M cattle." He turned back to the sheriff. "He also said that after some court thing settled, the moratorium on Bar-M cattle would likely be reinstated." Rowdy narrowed his eyes. "And what court case do you think that's likely to be, Sheriff?"

The sheriff stood straighter and scowled at Rowdy. "I have no idea what you're talking about, Mr. Waters or what you think Luke would have to do with any of it."

Nobody had noticed an additional car drive up and stop until Callie joined the group. She gasped when she saw the blood on Rowdy's shirt. "What the hell is going on here, sheriff? Are you hurt Mr. Waters?"

"It's not my blood," Rowdy said. "It's—"

"I'd wager you know exactly what is going on here, Miss Miller," the sheriff growled. "Deputies, take these two into custody as well for conspiracy to steal cattle."

"What?" Rowdy and Callie gasped at the same time.

✣ 16 ✣

C ody took the keys to their cars and promised to get them
back to the ranch. He also took Mr. Carlisle's number
and promised to call the family attorney and explain what was
going on. Wheeler's men unloaded the cattle and Cody made
certain they got photos of the brands to prove the cattle being
stolen were Miller cattle.

Luther and the other ranchers stayed with Cody until the
truck was unloaded to make certain none of the beef bore
their brands.

"What do you make of all this, Cody?" Luther asked.

"I think the sheriff might have it right," one of the other
ranchers said, "and that pretty redhead has that man wrapped
around her finger—"

" or pussy-whipped so bad he'd do anything she asked him
to," said one of the others. "I know I'd have a hard time
refusing that if I had my cock between her legs on a regular
basis."

They all laughed except Cody. "I think all of you know
Miss Callie," he snapped, "and that she's not that kind of
person. Furthermore, none of you know Rowdy and know
he's a man of great integrity who'd never be involved in cattle

rustling just to tarnish the name of another." He curled his nose. "But you all know that bastard Lucas Jones and how he's claimed he should be the one running Miller Ranch because he's the illegitimate git of ol' man Miller and his whore Doris Jones." Cody spit on the ground. "I think he tried to kill Miss Callie after she fired his ass by cutting her brake line and furthermore," he added with a raised brow, "I think it's likely he killed her parents by doing much the same to their car." He shook his head. "Nobody gave it much thought back then, but I went over to Samuelson's Salvage and asked them to find Morgan's car, and give it a good going over to see if anything had been tampered with."

"And?" Dan Willoby from Willoby Ranch asked with a raised brow.

Cody shook his head. "Still waiting to hear from him."

"Vick Samuelson is a good man," Luther said. "If there's anything to be found, he'll find it."

"I know Lucas has had a hard-on about this ranch since he was a kid and he had a right to the hard-on," Tim Turner from Turner Beef said, "but I have a hard time believing he'd be alright stealing from the rest of us." He shook his head. "Why?"

"Money," Luther said. "It's always about money where Lucas is concerned. He never had it when he was a kid, thought he deserved it as the son of Morgan Miller, and is going after it now with that lawsuit against Callie."

"Which he doesn't have an ice cube's shot in hell to win," Tim said. "He's been down that road before and was shot down every time. He's a bastard and bastards can't inherit their father's property if there was legal offspring to inherit."

Dan scratched his head. "My wife's sister works at the courthouse in Missoula," he said, "and she heard some of the clerks talking. It seems ol' Lucas has some new evidence that just might have him livin' in that big ranch house after all."

"What sorta evidence?" Cody demanded.

Dan chuckled. "Why? You worried Luke is gonna fire you and toss you and your pregnant bitch out of that nice new house Callie fixed up for you to live in when she gave you his job?"

Cody pushed forward and bumped chests with Dan. "I earned that job, Dan, after working on that ranch since I graduated high school fifteen years ago."

Dan grinned. "The same school Callie graduated from?" he asked. "How often did you tap that, Cody? Does your little squaw know you used to fill your boss's holes before you filled hers?"

Tim and Luther laughed. Luther slapped Cody's back. "Don't worry, Cody. If Lucas ends up with the Miller and tosses you out, I'll make sure you have a place on my ranch."

"Yah," Cody sighed, "but not as your foreman for the money Callie is paying me with a place on the ranch for Zena to live."

Luther's face lost its smile. "I like you, Cody, and have watched your progress over the years with Lucas as your foreman, but in my opinion, Callie jumped the gun, giving you the foreman job. You're a capable hand, but you're not ready for the foreman job yet. Maybe in five more years after you've earned it, but you have a lot to show me before that."

"I suppose that's where you and Callie differ," Cody said with a raised brow.

"How's that?" Luther said.

"Callie's been watching me work for the past fifteen years on this ranch and knows my worth to Miller Ranch as a foreman. I've already proven myself to her even though you might not have any faith in her opinion as a woman owner."

Luther smiled. "Unlike that asshat Dan, I've known Callie Miller all her life and if any person, man or woman, knows ranching, it's her and if she thinks a person is ready to Foreman, I'd be hard-pressed to speak against her." He offered his hand to Cody. "If Lucas wins this ranch from Callie," he said,

"I'd be proud to have you as my foreman at my Pine Mountain Ranch with the ranch house at your disposal for you and your bride to live in."

Cody took the man's hand and smiled. "I really appreciate that, Luther, but hopefully Callie's lawyer is as good as she thinks he is, and we can stay right where we are."

Luther nodded. "I hear that. I'm sure your wife wants to stay close to her family here near the reservation with the little one on the way."

"That she does," Cody said, "and she's hoping to see Lucas charged and convicted for her aunt's murder."

"Do you honestly think Lucas Jones could do a thing like that?" Luther asked. "I've known the man all my life and I just don't see him doing something like that to an old woman like Rita."

Cody shrugged. "He told Callie he drowned her little brother to get him out of the way and wanted to get at Callie," he said, "and I've worked with Lucas long enough to know he doesn't let anything, or anyone stand in his way when he wants something."

Luther shook his head. "But beat and strangle a poor old woman like that who'd cooked his meals for years the way Rita had and kill a helpless little boy? I just can't see it."

"You've never seen the man go after something he really wanted," Cody said. "I saw him go bat shit crazy on a guy at an auction once when the guy kept outbidding him on a pickup he wanted."

"But he didn't kill him did he?"

Cody furrowed his brow. "No, but he sent the guy a coke laced with ipecac and the guy left the auction puking his guts out and Lucas got the pickup."

"Jeez," Luther gasped with his face turning red, "that was Lucas that did that?"

Cody's face paled. "You were the guy bidding against him?"

"I sure as hell was," Luther said, "and I spent three days in the hospital trying to figure out what happened to my damned stomach. It scared my poor Emma half to death with worry after she lost her pops to stomach cancer the year before."

"I'm really sorry about that, man, and Lucas thought it was really funny. He still tells that story at poker games to warn guys off who are trying to bluff him."

Luther clenched his fists. "Maybe I'll get me some of that ipecac and join the next game."

Cody grinned. "Miles Perry's place next Friday at seven."

"I'll be there with bells on," Luther said. "Thanks, kid."

⚜

"Phone, Mr. Wheeler," his receptionist said when she stuck her head in the door. "It's a Skip Martin, one of your drivers, and he says it's important about Mr. Kirkman and the job you sent them out on today."

"Well, take a—"

"He won't leave a message, Mr. Wheeler. I already tried to get him to leave a message, sir, both times he called."

Wheeler punched the flashing light on the phone. "This is Wheeler," he growled. "What's so damned important you couldn't leave a message with Jennifer?"

"What?" he gasped, and his eyes went wide. "Kirkman is dead? Very well, I'll take care of it and get you out of there." He hung up the phone and pushed the intercom button. "Get my lawyer down to Miller's Crossing to get our men out of jail down there," he yelled at Jennifer, "and then get that asshole, Lucas Jones, in here."

"Yes, sir," she said without question.

An hour later Jennifer ushered Lucas Jones into Mr. Wheeler's office. "What's up, Wheeler?" he asked before dropping into one of the chairs in front of the man's desk.

"Well, it seems everything went to hell on the Miller

Ranch and my man Kirkman is dead along with one other and the rest are locked up down there."

"And you need me why?" Lucas asked.

"I need you to get down there and clean up that damned mess, Lucas. This whole thing was your idea in the first place, and I expect you to be the one to clean it up."

Lucas's eyes went wide. "How am I supposed to clean up Kirkman's mess?"

"I have no damned idea," Wheeler yelled and leaped to his feet, "but get back down there, collect my damned truck, fill it with cattle, and bring it back here."

Lucas glanced out the window at the darkening sky. "It'll be dark by the time I get back to Miller's Crossing. You can't expect me to herd and load cattle in the damned dark all alone."

"Get some of your cowboy buddies down there to help you," Wheeler sneered. "I'm sure there is more than one who'd like to get even with that Miller cunt down there."

"You're probably right," Lucas said, rolling his eyes. "I'll see what I can come up with."

"That's a good boy," Wheeler said. "I knew I could count on you." He put his arm around Lucas's waist. "They told me the truck is still parked out there at that loading chute where they left it." He grabbed his coat and pulled him close. "Now get down there, get my fucking truck, and bring it back here to me filled with fucking cattle or I'll be sending you back there in little pieces your mama wouldn't recognize."

Lucas drove back to Miller's Crossing with his stomach doing flip flops. He gave what Wheeler said about his cowboy friends and stopped at a Stuckey to make some calls.

"Yah? Who the hell is this? It's eleven at night and I have to get up in the morning and go to work."

"Shut up and listen to me, Cody. It's Lucas and I need your help."

"Lucas? Lucas Jones? What the hell do you want with me?"

"I need you to help me with that truck, Cody. I gotta get that truck back to Wheeler filled with cattle or we're all in trouble here in Miller's Crossing."

"You want me to help you get the truck you sent here to steal Miller cattle in and send it back to that bastard Wheeler? Are you kidding me, Lucas? I can't help you steal Callie's cattle."

"You will if you want to keep your damned job, Cody, and keep your little squaw and papoose in that pretty little house by the pool. Because I'm gonna win my damned lawsuit and when I do and Miller Ranch is mine, I'm gonna throw you, your loose-lipped squaw, and your little half breed out on your asses and you'll never work on a damned ranch in Montana again asshole."

"Drop dead, Lucas, I'm not gonna help you steal Callie's cattle."

"Well, I'm gonna win that lawsuit next week, so you'd better have your fucking little cunt squaw pack up all your things because you'll be out on all your asses the minute the judge pounds the gavel and says Miller ranch belongs to me as the rightful Miller heir to the Miller Ranch with all the cattle on it.

"And again, Lucas, drop dead. When a judge says they're no longer Callie's cattle then maybe I'll help you steal them, but not until that day comes." He started to hang up but then put the receiver back to his head. "No, not even then, Lucas, because you're a murdering asshole and if you ever call my wife a squaw again, I'll come kill you myself." Cody slammed the receiver down. "Asshole son-of-a-bitch," he said into the empty room. "If you win that damned lawsuit, I don't want this job or the carriage house. I don't want to have anything more to do with Miller Ranch because there won't be a real damned Miller running it anymore."

❧ 17 ❧

The crowd at the Missoula courthouse filled every seat for the case of Jones vs Miller.

Sheriff Harris bent to whisper into Lucas's ear. "You drew Judge Harriet Cooper," he said with a smile. "She's gotta be one of the biggest liberals to wear a robe in this county. I think she'll see things your way, cousin, for sure of it."

The bailiff called the court to order and asked everyone to rise as Judge Harriet Cooper took the stand. Lucas took one look at the attractive black woman and snorted. "When did they start letting women judge men in this state?"

His lawyer shushed him with a glare. "Judge Cooper could very well see things our way, Lucas, so be respectful—and quiet."

The judge pounded her gavel. "I understand I'm hearing the case of Lucas Jones against Callista Miller regarding the ownership of Miller Ranch today? Will the plaintiffs please stand?

Callie and Mr. Carlisle rose as well as Lucas and his attorney Damian Talley. The judge studied the group. "I see both of you are here with representation, but I'd like to hear from both of you personally before we get into the boring legal terms of the case. Mr. Jones, since you are the one who has brought this case before me, please explain to me why."

Lucas cleared his throat. "Why, ma'am?" I don't think I understand what you mean by why."

The judge frowned. "I simply want you to tell me, in your own words, why you've filed this suit against this young woman for the ownership of this ranch. Why do you think you should own it and not her?"

"I filed the suit, Judge, because that ranch should have come to me after her parents died." He grinned over at Callie then. "And now it's come to light that the greedy little whore wasn't even Morgan Miller's git in the first place."

There was an uproar in the courtroom and the judge had to pound her gavel to restore silence. "I'll have quiet in my courtroom," she told the crowd, "or I'll clear the room." She glared at Lucas. "And, Mr. Jones, I'll ask you to watch your language in my courtroom and speak respectfully about others here," she said with a glance at Callie. "Please explain your statement as to Miss Miller's not being Morgan Miller's 'git', sir."

Lucas took the old diary from his attorney. "I have it written right here in one of her mother's diaries that she got pregnant by another man while she was in college and then pawned the brat off on Morgan, so she could marry him and live like a damned queen up in that big house and spend his money."

"Bailiff," the judge said, "please bring me the diary so I can see the evidence for myself."

The tall, older man in a county uniform strode across the floor, took the diary from Lucas, and carried it back to the judge.

Damian Talley stood. "I marked the pertinent pages, judge with pink tabs."

Callie jetted to her feet then. "I think the most pertinent pages are about six or eight before the ones he probably marked, your honor," she called out, glaring across the room at Lucas. "The pages where my mother describes the rape she endured at that man's hands."

Lucas snorted. "I never once had to rape that little redheaded slut, judge. All I had to do was snap my fingers and she'd either go down on her knees with her mouth open or on her back with her legs spread wide."

The people in the seats gasped and murmured amongst themselves and the judge pounded her gavel again. "Quiet people," she warned, "I'm trying to read here."

The room settled down as Judge Cooper studied the diary. She began reading on the first page and her face changed from smiles to serious to horror-stricken, and then to smiles again as she read. She lifted her eyes to Lucas. "You were quite the ass, were you not, Mr. Jones?"

Lucas shrugged. "I was young and in love," he said. "Rachel was supposed to be my wife and then I'd have been the one to have raised my daughter over there and not my brother, Morgan."

"I think I'm gonna barf," Callie said to nobody in particular and earned a laugh from the gallery.

The judge looked up. "Has this diary been authenticated?" she asked.

"It's my mother's handwriting, your honor," Callie said. "I'm certain from what I read in the others that they were written by my mother, Rachel Miller."

"There are others?" the judge asked.

"About thirty in total, judge," Callie said. "Journaling was my mother's preferred method of therapy." Callie picked up another diary. "In this one, she talks about the day Lucas surprised her in her bath, dragged her from the bathroom, and raped her on my father's bed.

"Yah," Lucas said with a snarl, "and how she killed my child when she realized she was pregnant again."

"Which was her right under the law, Mr. Jones." The

judge noticed the sheriff sitting behind Lucas. "Sheriff Harris," she said, "do you happen to be in my courtroom today on official business?"

"No, Judge," he said, glancing at Lucas, "I'm just here in support of a friend."

"I see," she said with a sigh. "I hope that friend appreciates the fact that the statutes of limitation have made it impossible for me to charge him with the crimes of rape he perpetrated upon this poor woman."

The sheriff rolled his eyes. "It was hardly rape, judge," he said with a chuckle. "Like Luke said, Rachel was what you'd call easy and lots of guys I know put the hump into her more than once."

Callie's mouth fell open. "That's a lie," she screamed with tears welling in her eyes. Then she turned back to the judge. "Harris wouldn't arrest his cousin anyway, your honor. Lucas broke into my house the night he took that diary, he tried to rape me, and he murdered my housekeeper Rita Torrez." Callie wiped her eyes, took a breath, and continued. "There are plenty of witnesses who saw him on the ranch that night, but Sheriff Harris refused to investigate Lucas or believe any of us." Callie pointed at Lucas's face. "See that cut on his face? I did that when he had me pinned on my bed, telling me how he was going to enjoy my body even after he knew he was my biological father and how he drowned my little brother in a cattle trough to get him out of the way. He's a liar, a pervert, and a murderer."

The judge's eyes went wide, and her skin appeared paler as she glared at the sheriff. "Is all of that true, Sheriff Harris?"

The sheriff stood. "It's true her old housekeeper was found dead on the kitchen floor, but it could have been from natural causes, in my humble opinion, As for the rest of it, I'd say it's the ramblings of a drugged up girl with nothing better to do than try to stir up trouble."

"There was no autopsy performed on this housekeeper?" the judge asked.

"Her family was Cheyenne and refused an autopsy," the sheriff said.

"But the doctor at the scene said she'd been strangled," Callie told the judge.

The sheriff snorted. "Woods is hardly a doctor, your honor. He runs a vet clinic on the ranch and tends to cattle and horses—not humans."

"He took perfectly good care of me after someone cut my brake line and my car flipped into a ditch," Callie countered, "and the sheriff refused to investigate that as well since we all suspected Lucas was the one who did it."

The courtroom grew loud again, and the judge pounded her gavel to restore order. She turned to her bailiff. "John, will you call in one of the State Police Officers here in the building. I fear this is something they should be made aware of."

Cody Jackson stood then and cleared his throat. "I have something to add, Your Honor."

"Go ahead, young man, we may as well hear what everyone has to say here today."

"Yes, ma'am," he said respectfully and removed his hat. "There has been a great deal of cattle theft going on around here lately and Mr. Jones has been implicated in it as well." He paused for a minute. "And he was on the ranch the night Rita was murdered. He was at my house before it happened that night. My house is on the property just behind the main house where Rita and Miss Callie live.

"Cattle theft too?" the judge said, rolling her big brown eyes. "And were you aware of this as well, Harris?"

"I, umm,—" the sheriff mumbled.

"He was in the middle of a shootout with rustlers on Miller Ranch just a few days ago where two men were shot and killed," Cody said. "He knew about it and that Lucas was involved up to his neck in it, but he didn't do anything except let all the culprits go the next day and take the truck back to Free Wheeling Enterprises where it came from."

"It was a Free Wheeling truck that ran me off the road that day," Callie said.

"And you think Mr. Jones had something to do with that as well?"

"Miss Miller had been out drinking the night before." the sheriff said, scowling at Callie. "She made quite a scene at The Devil's Den when she fired Luke in front of everyone there. Then she went home with some stranger and spent the night in his bed. I'm certain her accident was nothing more than just that—an accident caused by a half-drunk, sleep-deprived pill-popper who over-corrected on the gravel road and lost control of her old, poorly maintained vehicle."

"Regardless," the judge said, "you believe Mr. Jones did something to your vehicle, Miss Miller?"

Callie shrugged. "I wouldn't put it past him. I fired him the night before because I found discrepancies in the books while he was my ranch foreman. He was stealing from me."

Lucas snorted. "Miller Ranch should be mine. It's my birthright. How could I be stealing from myself?"

"And explain to me," the judge said, "how you figure this ranch to be your birthright and not Miss Miller's."

Lucas grinned over at Callie. "Well, for one thing, my daddy was a Miller for certain. Morgan Miller, Sr."

"And did he officially recognize you as his son?" the judge asked.

"Ma'am?" Lucas said with his face twisted in confusion. "Well, he paid my mama five hundred dollars a month in child support. He wouldn't have done that if he didn't think I was his boy."

"And did you submit to the DNA test I requested?"

"I sure did, ma'am," Lucas said, nodding confidently as he turned to Callie. "Now you'll see, bitch, that I'm as much a Miller as you are."

The judge sat, studying papers in front of her. "I wouldn't go bragging quite yet, Mr. Jones."

"What?" he gasped with his face going pale.

According to this report from the state lab comparing your sample to that taken from the cadaver of Morgan Miller Sr. buried in the Miller family cemetery, you are not related to him in any way."

"But that's impossible," Lucas yelled. "My mama told me Morgan Sr. was my daddy and she wouldn't lie to me about something like that."

Callie began to laugh, and Lucas came unglued. "Don't laugh, bitch, because if I'm no Miller and have no title to that ranch then you're no Miller either."

"There you go getting ahead of yourself again, Mr. Jones," the judge said with an impish grin. "And did you submit to a DNA test, Miss Miller?"

"I did, Your Honor," Callie said with a nod, "but I really don't care what it said at this point because I know my daddy loved me even though I wasn't his blood and he still willed the ranch to me after my mama told him the truth about what had happened with Lucas." She smiled at the judge. "That's all that really matters to me."

Judge Cooper nodded. "As it should, young lady, as it should, but like Mr. Jones, you're getting ahead of yourself."

"Ma'am?" Callie said, glancing up at her attorney.

"I think your mama may have left a thing or two out of this diary, hun," she said with a grin, "because according to the state lab, you are a one hundred percent DNA match to the cadaver of Morgan Miller Jr. He was your biological father and not Lucas Jones, Miss Miller."

"You see," Lucas screamed. "I told you Rachel was a slut and spread her legs for practically any guy with a hard cock. She was supposed to be going with me, but she was screwing Morgan all that time."

"Bailiff," the judge called, "take control of this man and

remove him from my courtroom." She turned to Callie. "I rule in favor of Callista Miller in this matter. Miller Ranch belongs solely to her as the blood heir of Morgan Miller Jr. and his wife Rachel."

"Don't be ridiculous, Judge, that stupid bitch can't run a ranch." He began to laugh maniacally. "She can't even keep track of her damned cows, for Christ's sake."

Sheriff Harris tried to calm his cousin. "I'm sorry, Judge Cooper, but you've turned his world upside down today. He's always been certain he was a Miller. Now you've taken that away from him." He put his arm around his cousin and spoke softly to him.

"I couldn't take something the foolish man never had in the first place," the judge said. "This case is finished, and I would suggest Mr. Jones not bring any further suits to waste the court's time with."

With that, Lucas Jones snatched the pistol from the sheriff's holster and fired it into the plastered ceiling. Women in the gallery screamed and people ran for the doors. The bailiff grabbed the startled judge and rushed her through the door to her private office. When he returned with his gun in his hand, Lucas shot him as well.

Callie screamed and Lucas turned in her direction. "Now I can get my revenge on the Miller clan once and for all," he said, leveling the weapon at the redhead. "I'm gonna kill you this time, Rachel for being the two-timing slut I always knew you were. You swore to me and to Mama that you and Morgan Jr, were nothing but friends, but you lied like you always lie."

As Lucas cocked the pistol, something blurred through the air and sounded with a thunk as it stopped in Lucas's chest where his heart beat. He gasped and crumpled to the floor, clawing at the elk-horn handle of a Cheyenne hunting knife. "That was for Rita and young William, asshole," Rowdy said as he leaped over the railing to take a trembling Callie into his arms. "They're avenged now," Rowdy said as he kissed the top of Callie's head, "and Rita can rest easy beside her husband George."

The sheriff rushed around to pry his gun from the hand of his cousin and return it to his holster. "I'm afraid you're under arrest now, Mr. Waters," he said, as he unclipped handcuffs from his belt.

"What the hell for?" Callie demanded.

"For the murder of Lucas Jones," the sheriff said with a smug look on his face. "Everyone here saw it."

Judge Cooper along with three Montana State Troopers rushed into the room as the sheriff cuffed Rowdy's hands behind his back. "What the hell happened in here?" the judge demanded.

"I'm arresting the man who murdered my cousin," the sheriff said. "You may have taken his Miller name from him, but he was still a Jones."

"Judge," Callie pled, "Rowdy saved my life. Lucas was about to shoot me when he threw that knife at him. I'd be dead if not for him and that worthless excuse for a sheriff knows it."

"Gentlemen," she said to the troopers, "arrest this useless piece of human excrement and get him out of my sight."

"You got no right to have me arrested, bitch," the sheriff yelled as the troopers took his gun and badge.

Judge Cooper pointed a manicured finger in his face. "I do and I did, so get used to it."

"What should we charge him with?" one of the troopers asked.

The judge shrugged. "I don't care," she said with a giggle. "Get creative if being a huge piece of useless slime won't hold up in court try dereliction of duty or conspiracy to cover up a murder in the case of this young lady's housekeeper or rape. Take your pick."

They cuffed the sheriff and led him away. "You're free to

go, young man," the judge said as she unlocked his cuffs, "with my deepest thanks for ridding the Earth of this other piece of filth who killed one of the sweetest men you'd ever want to know," she said, glancing down at the body of her dead bailiff.

"And one of the sweetest women," Callie said.

18

Two weeks after the court case ended and Lucas Jones was cremated there was a Sunday Supper of celebration on Miller Ranch. Zena and the Torrez clan from the reservation cooked an amazing meal of carne asada, Indian Fry Bread, and seasoned tomatoes, onions, and peppers from Rowdy's garden. The family members wore traditional Cheyenne costumes and danced and sang in honor of Rita's spirit being avenged.

Rowdy was praised and George presented him with a new knife and beaded sheath he'd made himself. "You are our brother now, Rowdy and I'd be a proud man if you'd wear this knife."

"It's beautiful, George," Rowdy said as he studied the polished steel. "You made this yourself?"

George smiled with pride. "My father and uncles taught me bladesmithing," he said. "It's an old Cheyenne profession in our family."

"It's something I've always wanted to learn," Rowdy said. "I'm a bit of a picker and a scrapper and have lots of old steal laying around."

George slapped Rowdy's back. "Then as my new brother, I'd be proud to teach you."

Rowdy beamed. "Really?"

"And have him teach you to make cabinets, cousin," Zena called. "I know your wife would appreciate some like he can make."

George shushed her with a wave of his hand and took the meat that smelled of cumin, garlic, and lime juice from the grill. Zena added more of the yeasty fry-bread to her platter, took the pan of oil from the grill, and followed her cousin and Rowdy to the table.

Callie stood at the French doors leading into the kitchen, watching her employees and friends getting ready to enjoy another meal together. She didn't think things could get any better.

"Come on, Cal," Rowdy called to her as he set a cardboard box on the table and began passing around pint jars of something, "or you're gonna miss this wonderful feast."

"What's that?" she asked as people began opening the jars.

"Salsa?" George said with one of the jars beneath his nose.

Rowdy nodded. "Made from the tomatoes, onions, and peppers in my garden," he said with pride. "I brought it down for Callie, but since it sorta went with the menu, I'll bring her some more from my pantry."

George tipped up the jar and let some of the chunky salsa run into his mouth. "This is really good, man. Where the hell you learn to cook like this?"

Rowdy smiled. "My mama taught her boy how to survive from the garden," he said, "and not do without the finer things in life. You should taste my ragu."

"Cool," Cody called from down the table, "spaghetti next Sunday with lots of garlic bread."

Everyone praised Rowdy's salsa on the fry-bread tacos, and he promised to bring jars of his ragu sauce for the next supper. "I'll probably be bringing my mama too," he whispered in Callie's ear as people began to leave the table.

"Your mother is coming?" Callie asked with her eyes wide.

"It's why I can't stay tonight," he said with a raised brow. "I have a couple of big projects up at the cabin to finish before she gets here."

Now it was Callie's turn to raise a brow. "Big projects, huh?"

Rowdy grinned. "I promised ragu, so I guess I'm gonna have to make some."

"How's the greenhouse coming along?" Callie asked as she began to gather plates to carry to the kitchen.

"Since Cody volunteered to stain and seal the carriage house, I thought I'd have plenty of time to get it all together, but them Mama called and said she had a hankerin' to see Montana and all the real cowboys, so I had to put the greenhouse on hold for a bit."

"Don't wait too much longer," she warned with a smile, "or the first snow will fly, and you won't have it up. I can't wait to see what else you've done with the place," Callie said. "It seems like you've changed it so much every time I'm up there. You know I don't think you should be spending all your money to fix up my cabin, don't you?"

Rowdy put his arm around her. "As long as I'm living there, I think it's my responsibility to make it livable for me." He shrugged his broad shoulders. "And anyhow, I've told you before, I'm a picker and a scrapper. I don't spend a lot on anything if I can find it and repurpose it."

Callie stacked dishes by the sink. "Now you have my imagination running wild," she said with a giggle. "I'm gonna have to come up and see what you've done now."

Rowdy smiled in anticipation. "Come up with me now and spend the night," he whispered in her ear, pulling her lithe body into his.

"Wish I could," she said with a sigh, "but I've got ranch

business to discuss with Cody and the boys before they head out tonight. I think Zena made flan for dessert. You should stay for that at least."

Rowdy glanced at the refrigerator where he knew the sweet treat cooled. He kissed Callie's cheek. "Nah, I'd better head out, feed Princess and the chickens, and then hit the hay. I have a lot going on tomorrow." He kissed her mouth this time and lingered, his tongue playing with hers. "Tell everyone bye for me," he said and left the ranch house with a throbbing in the thickness between his thighs. The woman drove him mad and she knew it.

He'd finally opened up to his mother about Callie in a long conversation after everything that had happened in the courtroom and that was when Sherri told him she'd already booked a flight to Montana to come visit her boy. Rowdy knew it was because his mama wanted to meet this girl who had her son so tied up in knots he'd kill to protect her. She knew this was no simple schoolboy crush and she wanted to meet her.

Callie dressed for cool weather since the mountain was so much cooler than down on the ranch. She also filled her pocket with slices of dried apple for Princess. Callie loved late summer in Montana. The days were still warm, the evenings cool, and the colors of the trees on the mountains were beginning to change. Soon they would be ablaze with shades of yellow and red, warning every one of the snows soon to come and the high winds that would strip away all color except green, gray, and white as winter took hold with her icy talons.

For now, however, the sun shone bright in the blue Montana sky, the fields were green and dotted with healthy beef, and the only snow dusted the highest reaches of the mountains around them. The cabin sat at roughly six thousand feet above sea level and could see snow any time after Labor Day with ease. Callie hoped Rowdy's projects didn't keep him from getting his greenhouse finished before then.

She smiled. The man certainly enjoyed his fresh produce and after tasting the salsa he'd brought, she knew he was handy in the kitchen. She looked forward to meeting the woman who'd raised him to be the sort of man he was.

When Callie got out of the car, she heard hammering coming from the rear of the cabin. She was about to walk back there when Princess bawled, and Callie made a detour to treat the calf with some of the dried apple slices. "You're getting so big, girl," Callie said with a giggle as the calf took the apple greedily from her fingers. "I still think he's mixing Miracle Grow in with your milk." The calf bawled for more apples, but Callie turned toward the cabin.

She walked inside to the aroma of Italian spices and a film of white dust on everything. "Damn, it smells good in here," Callie called out as she dropped her purse on the counter beside the sink. She smiled and shook her head. Her grandmother would have certainly approved of all these improvements. In her time here, dishes had been washed in a galvanized tub with water hauled from the creek and heated on the stove. Now there was an actual sink, and running water from faucets that gave you cold and hot. Electric lights lit the room and the dishes and food were stored safely in cabinets. Yes, her grandmother would have approved of all of this in her special sanctuary. Tears stung Callie's eyes as she thought about her beloved grandmother and how much she'd have loved all of this.

"Hey there," Rowdy said as he took the lid from the pot and stirred the contents. He offered Callie the spoon. "Taste this and tell me if you think it needs anything."

Callie took the wooden spoon. tasted the red sauce, and smiled. "Maybe just a little salt," she said and continued to lick the rest of the sauce from the spoon. "This is really good, Rowdy. Now I wish I had a plate of noodles to put some on."

She notices splotches of white plaster on his sleeves and

jeans. "What have you been doing now and what is this white dust all over everything?"

He took her hand and pulled her toward the bedroom. Since Mama was coming, I thought I'd better fix up somewhere for her to stay." He grinned. "I couldn't have her sleep on the couch and I certainly didn't want to, so," he said, stopping beside the toilet and pointing to a doorway where the window in the wall once was, "I added another bedroom and closed off the bathroom so there would be more privacy."

Callie's mouth dropped open. "You built on a bedroom?" She walked through the doorway to find a large empty space with a window in each wall and a set of French doors that opened onto a deck built around the hot tub. "This is unbelievable," she said as she walked out onto the deck and stared at the addition that looked as if it had been part of the original cabin. "How did you make it look like this?"

Rowdy smiled. "I told you I'm a scrapper and a picker," he said. "I found this big pile of board and batons at the scrap yard and thought they'd match the cabin perfectly, so I grabbed 'em up for next to nothing. Ole Carl was glad to have the space for something else. He said they came from an old cabin he and his son dismantled some time ago He even had a bunch of the old joists and such, so I didn't have to visit Home Depot for too much to put this whole room on," he said with a grin. The bedroom is twelve by twelve with an eight-foot deck around the hot tub and I had plenty of cedar shingles left in the barn from that project, so they match the rest of the house. All I've got left to do now is finish drywalling and then paint."

Callie wrapped her arms around his neck and kissed his mouth. "I can't believe you, Mr. Waters. You're amazing. How did you do all of this in just a couple of weeks?"

He grinned and bent his arm to make a muscle. Didn't I tell you that I actually came from Krypton and not Missouri?"

They walked back into the new bedroom space. "Don't

worry about furniture," Callie said. "There are a couple of old bedroom sets up in the attic. Pick the one you like, and I'll have a couple of the boys load it up and drive it up here for you."

"Thanks, Callie," Rowdy said with a relieved look. "I was wondering what I was going to do about that, but you pick the set you want to send up here. It's your stuff, not mine."

"Ok, when do you think you'll have it ready for furniture?"

Rowdy pulled her close, kissed her, and grinned. "If I don't get distracted probably in a couple of days."

The redhead kissed him back. "And when is your mother getting here?"

"I pick her up at the airport on Saturday," he said between kisses, "at ten in the morning."

"Then you'd better get to work, Mr. Waters, because that drywall isn't gonna hang itself." She smiled. "Should I bring Zena up to help you choose the paint colors?" Callie doubled over laughing at the horrified look that came over Rowdy's face.

❧ 19 ❧

Sherri Waters' visit was a great success. Rowdy hadn't seen his Mama since returning from Afghanistan two years ago before he traveled to Denver for rehab treatment at the VA hospital there.

"How in the name of heaven did you find this place, Rowdy?" his mother asked as they traveled up the steep, narrow road to the cabin. "You always complained about our place in Missouri being too remote and then you end up on a mountain top in Montana." She laughed and sucked down the last of her huckleberry shake. "This isn't bad," she said, "but certainly nothin' to write home about."

Rowdy smiled. "The huckleberries are sorta the thing here in Montana, Mama. They don't grow wild everywhere like they do up here."

Sherri smiled. "I guess ol' Doc Holliday liked 'em."

"I think that was just something they put in the movie, Mama. Doc Holliday was actually from Georgia and I don't know that he ever stepped foot in Montana."

They pulled up in front of the cabin and parked. Princess bawled for attention as soon as they opened the doors and Rowdy escorted his mother over to meet her.

"This is Princess, Mama," he said as he fed the calf slices of dried apple from his pocket.

"You'll give that baby the runs, feeding her all those apples," his mother scolded.

Rowdy laughed. "She's on a diet of grass and hay now that she's bitten the end of the last nipple off her bottle. Doc Woods told me when she did that it was time to ween her."

Sherri laughed and rubbed at the tip of her breast. "Yah, mine told me the same thing about you when you started getting those damned teeth."

He laughed and put an arm around her shoulder to walk her back to the cabin. "My garden is about finished now," he said, pointing to the wilted rows of plants. "been getting some hard frosts now and Callie says to expect snow up here before long."

Sherri raised a brow. "That's about the tenth time you've mentioned that girl's name, baby. When do I get to meet her?"

"She has a ranch to run, Mama," Rowdy said with a smile, "but for sure tomorrow when we go down for Sunday Supper with the hands from the ranch."

"You mean I'm finally going to get to meet some real cowboys?" she exclaimed. "What's that?" she asked, pointing to a collection of tall posts planted in the ground.

"If I ever get my shit together," Rowdy said, "it's gonna be my greenhouse."

Sherri studied the posts. "I thought greenhouses were more rounded," she said, "with plastic sheeting going over them."

Rowdy smiled. "You know I don't do things like everybody else, Mama. This greenhouse will have a shed roof with the back wall about a foot higher than the front and it will be covered in those clear corrugated hard plastic panels. Those will hold up better here than plastic sheeting the wind can rip off."

Sherri nodded. "Sounds like you've given it plenty of thought.

"Come on and let me show you the house." He pointed out the new roof on the barn. "My deal for reduced rent on this place was to do some repairs," he said, "but when Callie saw my work, she cut out the rent money altogether and even gave me a paying gig down on the ranch fixing up an old place for her new foreman to live in."

"I bet she did," Sherri said with a giggle.

"Mama," Rowdy scolded. "Callie is a good landlord and a good businesswoman. I think you're gonna like her."

They stepped up onto the porch. "If you like her, baby, I'm sure I'll like her too."

Rowdy unlocked the door and they stepped inside. Sherri stared around and smiled. "This is charming, Rowdy." She walked to the sink and ran a hand over a cabinet door, grinning. "I seem to recognize this design."

"Just like you taught me, Mama." He opened a cabinet door and took out a quart fruit jar. "My garden was good to me," he said, "and I got ten quarts of ragu, eleven pints of salsa, ten pints of tomatoes, ten of green beans, and six of corn." He smiled. "I probably could have put up more if I hadn't been taking stuff down to Miss Rita at the ranch for Sunday Suppers."

Sherri raised a brow. "Miss Rita?"

"She was Callie's housekeeper and she's dead now."

"It sounds like you cared about her, Rowdy, I'm sorry." Sherri kissed her son's forehead. "What happened to her? Natural causes?"

"Hardly," Rowdy said with a snort. "That guy I told you about at the courthouse killed her."

Sherri frowned. "Then I guess you got justice for her."

Rowdy took the knife George had made for him and handed it to his mother. "That's what her family says and now I'm officially a brother to the Cheyenne."

Sherri's eyes went wide as she smiled. "Hot damn, I get to meet real Indians too?"

Rowdy hugged his mother. "You're in Montana now, Mama, and this is about as close to the old west as you're gonna get."

Sherri ran a hand over the bent vine back of the couch. "I love this furniture," she said. "Where did you get it?"

"All the furniture in the cabin belongs to Callie," he said. "All this was out in the barn in pieces and I put it back together and made new cushion covers to match the curtains."

Sherri smiled. "I'm glad to see some of the things I made you learn as a boy have come in handy."

"I don't make clothes like you do, Mama, but I can handle a curtain hem and a seat cushion."

They stood laughing when there was a tap on the door and Callie came bursting in. She rushed past mother and son without a word, ran into the bathroom, and slammed the door.

Sherri stared into the dark room where the redhead had disappeared with her face twisted in confusion. "And that was?" she asked.

Rowdy smiled. "My landlord," he said. "Can't hold her coffee on that long bumpy road up the mountain." He picked up Sherri's suitcase. "Let me show you your room, Mama."

As they passed by the bathroom door, they heard gagging as Callie emptied her stomach into the toilet. Sherri looked up at her son with a raised brow. "Here's your room, Mama," Rowdy said and flipped on a light switch to illuminate a beautiful bedroom suite from the early 1940s with decorative geometric inlays of contrasting wood.

"This is beautiful, baby," she said as she dropped into an over-stuffed chair from the same time period. I feel like I'm in an old movie or something."

Rowdy opened the French doors leading out to the deck. "I don't know if you brought a swimsuit or not," he said as he lifted the cover from the hot tub, "but you're welcome to come out here and soak anytime you want to."

"My lord, child," she said with a giggle, "you might never get me back onto a plane for Missouri again with luxuries like this up here."

"You're welcome to stay for as long as you want, Mama, but we might get snowed in up here for weeks at a time if what I've been told is true."

Callie stepped into the room, wiping her mouth with a washcloth. "If you've been told what is true?" she asked with a weak grin.

Rowdy left his mother and rushed to Callie's side. "Are you all right, Cal?"

Callie nodded. "I'm fine, Rowdy. I guess something I ate last night didn't agree with me."

She offered her hand to Sherri. "I'm Callie Miller," she said. "Hasn't he done wonders with this old place?" Callie gestured around the room. "I still can't believe he built this whole room for you in only two weeks."

Sherri smiled up at her son. "He's a good son and always been pretty handy to have around."

"Well, you did a fine job raising him," Callie said. "He's a good tenant, a good employee, and a good friend."

Rowdy blushed. "Will you two cut it out before my damned head swells too big for my hat." He took Callie's hand. "You feeling up for some lunch? I have some hotdogs with all the fixin's."

Callie put a hand on her abdomen. I feel fine now," she said with an embarrassed grin. "Guess I'm gonna have to stop taking my suppers at Penny's Diner."

"I thought Zena cooked for you," Rowdy said.

"She usually does, but with Cody getting ready to take the boys out to brand, I've been sending her home early to spend time with him." Callie smiled. "You know how pregnant women are."

"Other than being indecisive about what color is supposed to go on what wall," Rowdy said as he collected the things for their lunch from the refrigerator, "no, I don't know much about pregnant women."

As he heated hotdogs on the iron flat top of the stove, Rowdy told his mother about painting the carriage house with Zena. They all laughed together and while Rowdy put together the condiments, Callie slapped her hand over her mouth and bolted for the bathroom again.

"What do you think is up with that?" Rowdy asked as they listened to Callie heave.

Sherri grinned. "How long have the two of you been … eh … intimate?" she asked, trying to keep a straight face.

Rowdy thought about it. Had it really been more than three months since their afternoon in the hot tub? "That's really none of your concern, Ma—" then he stopped when he got the gist of what his mother was implying. "I thought they only threw up in the mornings," he said with his face going pale.

Sherri snorted. "Most do," she said, "but with you, I puked like the devil right after supper for three damned months."

Rowdy paced around the table and then dropped into Callie's grandma's rocker. "Oh, my lord," he said with a sigh as he glanced up at his mother. "I don't know if I'm ready to be a father yet."

"And I'm too damned young to be a grandma," Sherri scolded as she ran her hand through her auburn hair, "but here we are. Didn't you two grown adults take the proper precautions?"

Rowdy was about to snap back at her when Callie came back from the bathroom with a washcloth over her mouth. "I'm sorry about that," she said. "I guess I'm gonna have to avoid the banana cream pie at Penny's from now on."

"Cream pie, huh?" Sherri said with a wink at her son.

"So, do you like your bedroom, Sherri?" Callie asked as she went back to the job she'd left behind. "Rowdy worked really hard on it to make it perfect for you."

"He did a beautiful job," Sherri said, trying to hold back the corners of her mouth from spreading into a grin. "And it will be useful when others get here too."

"Others?" Callie said. "Are you expecting more visitors, Rowdy?"

Rowdy glanced at his mother and then back to Callie. Should he just put it out there and ask her if she was pregnant? No, that was something she needed to sort out for herself. Maybe she didn't want children … maybe she didn't want his children. He'd let her make the decision as to when or if she told him. Hell, she might not even be pregnant at all and all the vomiting actually was due to a piece of Penny's banana cream pie.

"Oh, no, I'm not expecting anyone but Mama." He put the plate of hotdogs on the table and kissed the top of Callie's head. "Let's just steer clear of Penny's until she finds a new cook."

"Sounds like a plan," Callie said as she forked a dog from the plate and put it on a bun. "Zena asked me to pick up the cans of ragu for Sunday Supper tomorrow too." She smiled at Sherri. "I hope you're planning to join us. Everyone is really excited to meet Rowdy's amazing Mama after all the good things he's told us about you."

"I wouldn't miss my chance to meet real cowboys and Indians," Sherri said with a grin. "You bet I'll be there.

Callie bit into her dog. "Do you really support yourself selling produce at a farmer's market?"

Sherri smiled and rolled her eyes. "That and about a hundred other things. My big thing now is making dresses for the girls at the high school for their dances and such." She turned to Rowdy and smiled. "Homecoming is just around the corner and I have about a dozen orders to get back to when I get home." She winked at Rowdy again. "And then there are the dresses I make for the little girls. The Barbies in Jackson, Missouri are probably the best dressed in the state, by far."

Rowdy chuckled. "And don't forget about the Kens," he said. "Mama used to steal my GI Joes to dress up with her Barbies," he said. "My first sexual fantasies were about what Barbie and GI Joe were doing in that box alone together all week."

"Oh, my," Callie said and laughed.

Sherri slapped her son's shoulder. "Don't be ridiculous," she scolded her son, "Joe is always a perfect Military gentleman, just like you, and would never take advantage of a lady."

"I don't know, Mama," Rowdy said with a grin at Callie, "have you seen those knockers on Barbie and that cute round ass? I don't think Joe could hardly resist 'em when they're stuck in that dark box together all week."

Sherri shook her head with an embarrassed glance at Callie. "This is not the boy I raised," she said with a deep sigh. "Too many bad influences over there in Afghanistan is all I can figure."

Callie laughed. "You've never listened to bunkhouse talk then. I'm sure Cody and the rest of the boys have been educating him too."

Sherri smiled. "You have any boys my age workin' for you?"

"Mama," Rowdy exclaimed.

"Hey," Sherri said, "I'm old, but I'm not dead yet."

Callie laughed and Rowdy sat shaking his head. Only his Mama! But it was nice to have her at the cabin and she seemed to like Callie. He smiled at the two women in his life as they chatted and giggled together. Callie seemed to like his mama as well.

❦ 20 ❦

As Callie drove back down the mountain, she reflected on the day's occurrences. Her belly rolled, but she thought it was too many hotdogs with chips, pork and beans, and beer that brought it on. Had her throwing up like that hinted to Rowdy and his mother about her condition? Both had been reluctant to give her beer when she asked for one.

"Are you sure you want a beer, Callie?" Sherrie had asked when she'd gotten up to get one for herself.

"Yah," Rowdy had added, "you probably don't wanna be too juiced up driving down that steep road, especially now that the State guys have released Sheriff Harris and he has all his assholes gunning for us."

"You're right," Callie agreed with a sigh, "but hotdogs without a beer is like sacrilege. Just one," she begged, "and I'll sip it really slow."

Sherri stared at her son and then brought Callie the ice-cold Bud. "And just what did the two of you do to get into the crosshairs of this sheriff?" Sherri asked as she returned to her chair.

"Got his fat, lazy ass thrown into jail for not doing his job," Callie said.

"And I killed his murdering cousin," Rowdy added.

"Oh, that guy," Sherri said. "Sorry to bring up bad memories."

"It's all right, Mama," Rowdy said. "What's done is done, and we've been cleared by the State Police of any wrongdoing."

"But this sheriff is still holding a grudge. That can't be good." Sherri put another hotdog into a bun, slathered on mustard and catsup, and added chopped onions, relish, and tomato.

"I reckon, Rowdy, me, and most of the Miller Ranch employees have big targets on all our backs," Callie said. "Cody said him, and a couple of the boys have been pulled over twice now in Ranch vehicles."

Sherri shook her head. "Just one more good reason not to be drinking, young lady," she said with a glance at Rowdy.

They must have figured it out. Callie turned onto the blacktop and was glad to see no County squad car sitting at one of the regular speed traps. She'd be able to get to the Ranch road without worry. When she turned again, the three quart jars of ragu clinked together in the passenger's seat. She didn't think they'd need that many for tomorrow's supper, but Rowdy had insisted.

Callie's stomach rumbled as she passed the marker along Pike's Trail commemorating her parents and was happy her name hadn't had to be added to it. "Just calm down in there," Callie said in a calming voice to her unexpected passenger, "we'll be home in a minute."

When she'd missed her second period, Callie had purchased one of those home pregnancy tests and wasn't surprised when it had come back with a positive result. She'd been so worried about telling Rowdy, but maybe it wouldn't be so bad after all. He was a really good guy, but would he want to marry her? Did she really want to marry him? Rowdy had grown up without a father. Would he want his child to grow up without one too?

Sherri would never force a man to marry just because she carried his child. There had to be more to the relationship than that. But what about her parents? They'd married because Rachel was pregnant, and Callie knew there had been love between her parents though Morgan had been a philanderer like his father and enjoyed many lovers. Callie didn't think Rowdy was that sort of man, but she really didn't know him that well at all. For all she knew, Rowdy Waters could be a serial killer and for all he knew about her, she could be one too. They were going to need to sit down and have a serious discussion about a lot of things.

Rowdy still didn't know the first thing about ranching. How would he deal with all the social obligations involved? Morgan and Rachel had been social butterflies and Callie remembered the big holiday dinners with dancing to a live orchestra and picnics by the pool on Independence Day and Labor Day. They mixed with State, Local, and National politicians who had anything to do with the cattle business or land and water rights. Would Rowdy, the simple farm boy from Missouri be able to wrap his head around all of that? Would he even want to?

And then there was the matter of the Miller money. She wasn't a millionaire by any means, but the Miller Ranch holdings were probably valued well over that. She was certain her attorney would insist on a prenup and if it were any other man, Callie wouldn't balk, but Rowdy Waters was different. Callie didn't see him as a gold digger like some of the young men she'd dated in college who'd begun proposing marriage and their undying love as soon as they knew her pedigree. While she thought he appreciated the big house, Callie was certain Rowdy Waters would be happy to live his life in the cabin up on the mountain. She smiled as she parked the car in the garage. If truth be told, so would she.

Zena took the jars of ragu into her arms. "I hope this is as good as his salsa," she said. "I'll add some good prime beef to it, mushrooms, and black olives the way my Cody likes, and it will be great with garlic bread, a big salad, and what about dessert, Miss Callie?"

Callie smiled. "How about that lemon cream pie you make with the sorbet and cream cheese?" she said.

Zena nodded and her face lit up. "I've been meaning to try making one with the prickly pear sorbet but putting it in one of the chocolate pie shells. What do you think, Miss Callie?"

"That sounds delightful, Zena. I look forward to tasting it. Make certain you make enough for everyone to have a piece or two," Callie reminded, "so two or three of each flavor." Callie knew Zena was an imaginative cook but sometimes fell short of common sense.

Rowdy and his mother arrived at the ranch house about an hour before everyone else and Sherri, an avid home chef, stepped in to help Zena. The idea of the simple pies excited Sherri and she was eager to join in. "What an amazing kitchen this is," Sherri exclaimed, examining the stainless steel stove, double ovens, and professional refrigerator. "I feel like I'm in one of those master chef's kitchens on television."

"Miss Rachel, Callie's mama, and my Aunt Rita designed it back when Miss Callie was still in school," Zena said. "Miss Rachel, she liked to throw big parties for all the folks," Zena said, "and she wanted a kitchen big enough to work in."

"Well, this one certainly is," Sherri said with a smile.

Sherri made the garlic bread to Zena's instructions and then helped her to make the pies. "You're a good woman like Mr. Rowdy is a good man," Zena said with a smile. "I see where he gets it from."

A tall, tawny skinned man with broad shoulders walked up behind Zena, took her by the shoulders, turned her around, and kissed her cheek. "And how is my best girl today?" he asked before patting her expanding belly. "And how is my handsome grandson doing in there?"

"Oh, Daddy, please," Zena said, brushing her father's work-worn hands away. "You're embarrassing me."

"Why would you be embarrassed, girl?" He glanced at Sherri and smiled. "Are they hiring white women to work in the Miller Ranch kitchens now?" he asked in a snide tone. "There won't be any work for our women off the reservation soon."

Zena glanced at Sherri and rolled her eyes. "Daddy, this is Sherri Waters, the mother of Mr. Rowdy come to visit him from Missouri. Sherri, this is my father Nathan Clearwater, chief, or as they prefer to call it now, Council President of the Flat Rock Cheyenne people."

Sherri offered her hand. "It's very nice to make your acquaintance, sir."

Nathan stared at Sherri before taking her hand. "Since my nephew has seen fit to name your son our brother, then I suppose I should welcome you as a sister, Mrs. Waters." He wrapped his strong arms around Sherri. "Be welcome, sister." He hugged her before turning and stalking away to the patio.

"Well, that was intense," Sherri said as she watched him go.

"Rita was his favorite sister," Zena said. "It's hard for him to walk back into this house where she was murdered." She took a deep breath. "Though my cousins and I are grateful Mr. Rowdy found justice for her by killing that terrible Mr. Lucas."

"I gather your father doesn't feel the same way."

Zena shrugged her shoulders. "Daddy is old school," Zena explained. "He thinks it should have been him to throw that knife into Lucas's heart, not a white man."

"I think I can understand that," Sherri said as she worked on the pie filling. "If it had been my sister, I think I'd have wanted to be the one to end the bastard's life who killed her."

Zena nodded. "Like Mr. Rowdy, I think you have the soul of a Cheyenne."

"How are things going in here, ladies?" Callie asked when she came into the kitchen.

"Are you feeling better today?" Sherri asked with a secret grin on her face as she put pies in the freezer to firm up.

Callie put her hand on her belly. "Much better today, thank you, but we have a hungry crew out here. Are we about ready to serve?"

Sherri opened the oven and pulled out a foil-wrapped package. "I think the bread is ready," she said, inhaling the garlicy aroma of the oven air.

"You can take out the bowls of salad," Zena told her. "I just dressed them all with Italian today."

Callie nodded as she picked up one of the clear glass bowls willed with mixed greens, glistening with Italian dressing. Sherri unwrapped the foil and placed sliced, crusty garlic bread onto trays.

"Miss Callie has been sick?" Zena leaned in to whisper to Sherri.

Sherri grinned. "Nothing that won't pass in about another six months or so," she said, patting Zena's baby bulge.

"Oh," Zena said with a grin. "Is Mr. Rowdy happy about it?"

"I don't think he's had the time to process it all yet, and she hasn't exactly told him either."

Zena nodded. "Miss Callie might have a hard time doing that after what happened to her over there in that war."

"You mean her hand?" Sherri asked.

"No," Zena said, shaking her head. "Aunt Rita told me that terrible man over there who took her captive got her pregnant and then took her hand when she wouldn't give him her grandmother's ring."

Sherri's face went pale. "That's terrible. What became of the child?"

"She saw old Doc Woods when she got home, and he did one of his D&Cs on her."

Sherri raised a brow. "Oh, I see." Sherri wondered if her son knew about that.

They walked out onto the patio and found empty seats. Zena sat beside her husband and Sherri beside Nathan Clearwater.

"How are you doing, Mama?" Rowdy asked as he bent and kissed her cheek.

"Great, baby," Sherri said. "I'm having dinner on a real Montana ranch with real cowboys and Indians," she said with a nervous glance at Nathan. "What more could a simple woman from Missouri ask for?"

Rowdy walked to Callie and took the seat beside her and people began filling their plates with salad and spaghetti covered in Rowdy's ragu enriched with good Montana beef. They filled their glasses with sweet red wine or beer and enjoyed their meal. The plates of bread emptied quick and Sherri asked if she should go to the kitchen and make more.

Nathan patted her hand and chuckled. "There's no need, sister. They'll fill their bellies with what is left."

Sherri smiled back. "And there is pie for dessert."

They finished their dinner and Sherri helped Zena and Callie to clean up afterward. Callie had to excuse herself once with her hand over her mouth and Sherri and Zena grinned at one another. "Mine was always in the morning," Zena said with a giggle when Callie returned, "or if I smelled bacon frying."

"With Rowdy mine was always in the evening after I ate my supper." She smiled at Callie. "It'll pass soon enough."

Callie rolled her eyes and dropped into one of the chairs at the table. "You know then?"

Sherri smiled. "Just an educated guess, really."

"And Rowdy?" Callie asked hesitantly. "Does he know?"

"Not my place to tell him," Sherri said with a slight shrug.

"Especially if there was nothing to tell." She winked at Zena. "So, is there something to tell?"

Callie released her breath. "I'm pregnant," she said. "Probably about two months along if my estimations are correct."

"And when did you plan to tell Rowdy about this?" Sherri asked.

"When I felt the time was right," Callie said.

Sherri, along with most of the others sleeping in the ranch house that night were jolted awake by a loud pounding on a door. "Callie Miller," Rowdy yelled, "I wanna know if you're pregnant with my child and I want to know now."

Nathan rolled over beside Sherri. "Perhaps my foolish nephew wasn't wrong about calling your son a brother after all," he said with a sleepy chuckle. "It takes a brave man to confront a woman like that in her own house."

Sherri snuggled into the man's side. "That's my boy," she whispered, "brave, but sometimes incredibly stupid."

Callie wasn't asleep when the pounding on her bedroom door began. She smiled and pushed the blankets aside when he made his demands.

"You have something to discuss with me, Mr. Waters?" she said when she opened the door and pulled him inside.

Rowdy 's face paled. "Are you pregnant with my baby, Callie?"

Callie pulled him into the room and shut the door. "Yes, but the whole house doesn't need to be privy to our business, Mr. Waters."

"Please, Callie," Rowdy said, taking her hands in his, "I need to know."

"And if I am?" Callie asked.

"We can marry and give the child a legitimate beginning in his life," Rowdy said.

"This child will have a name, Mr. Waters," Callie said. "He'll have the Miller name and everything that comes along with it."

"Is that so?" Rowdy asked. "Do you really want to raise that child without a father with everyone his age sniggering behind his back because he was born on the wrong side of the sheets?" Rowdy stared down into her bright green eyes. "I grew up that way, Callie, and I won't have that for my child. I'll marry his mother and save him all of that misery."

Callie pulled her hands from his. "And what sort of life would that child have with parents who don't love one another?" she demanded. "You've never said once that you loved me."

Rowdy's mouth dropped open. "I believe I've said more than once how much I love makin' love to you."

Callie rolled her eyes. "That isn't quite the same, Mr. Waters. I'll not marry a man who doesn't love and respect me." She took a deep breath. "My parents had love, I think, but there was no respect between them. Daddy screwed around the way his daddy did and my mother spent her time spending his money on fancy parties and fancy clothes to wear to 'em."

"But at least your daddy married your mama when she told him she had you in her belly," he said. "Mine wouldn't even give me his name."

"Are you ashamed of your name, Mr. Waters? I think your mother did a fine job with you and you didn't need that man's name to make you a good man."

"And just how did you feel for that week or so that you thought Lucas Jones was your father, Callie?" Rowdy asked. "Tell me how it felt to think you were a bastard and then tell me you'd want that for our child."

"It wouldn't be the same and you know it, Rowdy," Callie said. "I'd love this baby the way your mother loved you and it will want for nothing here on Miller Ranch."

"Maybe everything that Miller Ranch has to offer is most what I'd want to save him from."

"And just what's that supposed to mean?" Callie asked indignantly.

"Too much money and too many things can spoil a kid, Callie, and I'd not have that for my child."

As Callie opened her mouth to refute his statement, the window behind her shattered and Callie flew forward with a grunt, across her bed. Bright red blood began to bloom on her sleep shirt and Rowdy screamed and took her into his arms, "Callie. Help, somebody, Callie's been shot."

Nathan Clearwater followed by Sherri was the first into the room. Nathan, of course, should have been spending his night with Zena in the carriage house but had opted to spend his night in the guest room with Rowdy's mother instead.

"What the hell happened?" Nathan demanded as he took in the scene. Before becoming Council President, Nathan had been the Tribal Police Chief on the Reservation and possessed a rudimentary knowledge of forensics and investigative technique.

"Callie and I were having a conversation," Rowdy said, holding the unconscious woman in his arms, "when the window shattered, and she went sailing across the bed."

Sherri, who'd been in nursing school when she got pregnant with Rowdy, stepped in and took charge. "Let go of her, baby," Sherri said, "we need to get that bleeding slowed down. Somebody get me towels from the bathroom and call 911 for Christ's sake, so we can get her to a hospital."

One of the hands and his wife were staying in one of the other guest rooms and they ran across the patio to collect Cody and Zena from the carriage house where the party was still going strong. "Oh, my God," Zena screamed when she saw the blood covering Callie. "I'll run get Mr. Mak," she shouted.

"Just calm down, honey," Cody said, pulling his pregnant wife close, "I'll run get Mak. You just sit down and don't get too worked up. It's not good for the baby."

Zena's big brown eyes darted from Callie to Rowdy, and then to Sherri, who pressed towels onto the wounds in Callie's shoulder. "Baby," she muttered. "Will this hurt Miss Callie's baby?"

"Not if we can get the bleeding under control," Sherri said. "When is that damned ambulance gonna get here?" she yelled at nobody in particular.

"Cody went for Mr. Mak," Zena said. "He's a doctor who lives at the clinic."

"He's a vet," Rowdy clarified, "but his old man is a medical doctor and he seems to know his stuff."

Sherri rolled her eyes as she pressed more towels on Callie's wounds. "Probably as good or better than some I've known back in Missouri."

Mak rushed into the room with his bright blond hair loose and Rowdy suspected Cody had roused the man from his bed. They went through all the questions about what had happened again, and Sherri moved aside for Mak to inspect Callie's wounds. She also went into describing the injury as she'd been taught in nursing school while doing an ER rotation.

The bullet appears to have gone through and through, doctor and her clavicle feels like it's been shattered by the impact. I applied pressure to the wounds with towels as they were the best sterile dressings I could find." Sherri took a breath. "I asked that someone call 911 for transport, but they went for you instead. Oh, and," Sherri said with a glance at her son, "she's pregnant—eight to ten weeks she thinks."

"Thank you, nurse," Mak said with a grateful nod as he took his cell phone from his pocket and punched in a number. "Hey, Dad, I need you out at the ranch. Someone's shot Callie." He listened for a few minutes. "Yah, a through and through in the right shoulder, but her clavicle is shattered and she's gonna need surgery. I'm gonna move her over to the clinic, start an IV, and take some X-rays."

"Nurse," he said to Sherri, "can you get her prepared for transport? I have a gurney downstairs."

"It's just Sherri," she said with a grin. "I had my LPN

years ago, but I let it lapse because I hated working in hospitals."

"And she made more money sewing Barbie clothes to sell at the flea market," Rowdy added.

"And I had a rambunctious boy to look after, which made it difficult to do rotating shifts at a hospital."

"Rowdy," Mak asked, "can you carry her down the stairs to the gurney?"

"What the," Callie mumbled as he lifted her from the bed. "What happened?"

"Not sure yet, baby," Rowdy said, "but we're taking you over to Mak's clinic now."

Callie began to weep. "It hurts, Rowdy. It hurts so bad."

"I know, baby, but Mak will give you something for the pain when we get you to his clinic." Tears stung Rowdy's eyes to see her in so much distress. He kissed the top of her head. "I love you, Callie Miller."

"I love you too, Mr. Waters, and I'd be proud to be your wife."

The State Police arrived while Callie was in surgery. Rowdy explained again about their private discussion, the window shattering, and Callie flying across the bed. When one of them asked if there was anyone who might be holding a grudge against, Miss Miller, Rowdy told them the long drawn out story about what had happened with Lucas Jones and the lawsuit.

"That why you called us and not Sheriff Harris about this?" one of them asked with his face struggling to keep the grin from his lips.

"Something like that," Rowdy replied as he watched the troopers examine the shattered window in Callie's room and then pry a slug from the wall.

"This is a bullet from a high powered hunting rifle," one of them said as he dropped the mangled pellet into an evidence bag. "You have any idea who could have made a shot like that in the dark?"

Nathan Clearwater cleared his throat. "Doris Jones could have," he said from where he stood in a dark corner of the room.

"Lucas's mother?" Cody said with his brow furrowed. "She'd have to be pushing eighty by now."

"Yah," Nathan said, "but the old bird is a hell of a shot with that Remington of hers. I've chased her and her white supremacist poaching buddies off the Reservation I don't know how many times, taking elk and antelope out of season." He took a deep breath. "I'd bet ya, if ya looked in her damned freezer and that asshole Sheriff Harris's as well, you'd find 'em full of poached animals from my Reservation."

"Thank you, gentlemen," one of the troopers said. You've given us plenty to look into for this and we hope Miss Miller makes a full and quick recovery."

The State Troopers left, and Rowdy found himself alone in Callie's room with Nathan.

"I think I'll head on back to bed now, brother," the Cheyenne Council President said. "Your mother is a fine woman and I hope you're not—"

Rowdy put a hand up to stop the man. "My mama's sex life is none of my business, Nathan. She's a grown woman and can sleep with whoever she pleases, whenever she pleases without my consent or approval."

"Oh, well, good night then," the old Indian said, fondling his braided black hair as he scooted out the door to return to his guest room down the hall.

The following morning, Rowdy woke to the aroma of bacon frying. He dressed in clean jeans and a t-shirt before venturing down the stairs to find Zena, her father, and his mother all dressed and sipping coffee.

"I'm going over to Mak's to check on Callie," he said as he took the cup of coffee Zena offered him.

Zena poured another cup and fitted it with a plastic lid. "Here," she said, shoving the cup into his hand, take this one to Miss Callie. She says Mr. Mak makes the worst cup of coffee in the county."

"Thanks, Zena, I'm sure she'll appreciate it."

Rowdy left the ranch house carrying the two cups of coffee, sipping his as he walked toward the vet's clinic. He'd wanted to stay there with her that night, but Mak had sent him away, saying Callie would be sleeping all night and that he'd be much more comfortable in a bed in the ranch house than in a chair by her bed.

Rowdy entered the clinic through the unlocked back entrance and made his way to Callie's room, where he stood staring at her from the doorway. Her tanned, freckled face was pale, and her shoulder was heavily bandaged. An IV line ran into her arm and another tube into her nose.

"You might as well go in," Mak said from behind him. "She's been asking for you."

"How's she doing, Mak?" Rowdy asked. "And please don't sugar coat it for me. Are she and the baby—"

"They're both fine," Mak said. "She lost a lot of blood, but thanks to your mother's quick action, not enough to cause fetal distress during the surgery to repair her shoulder bone that was shattered by the bullet." He glanced at Callie and smiled. "I put in a feeding tube, which she's going to hate, but without the use of either hand to feed herself, she needs it."

Rowdy glanced at the cup of coffee in his hand. "Can you put this through that tube as well? You know how she is if she doesn't get her caffeine fix in the morning."

Mak chuckled. "I know, and she hates my coffee."

"You know I can hear you, right?" Callie mumbled and turned her head on the pillow to glare at them.

Rowdy went to her side. "Zena sent you coffee," he said with a grin.

"Thank God," she said but gasped in pain when she

reached for the cup with her injured arm. "I guess I'm going to need a little assistance with that."

Rowdy popped off the lid off the cup and put it to her lips. Callie took a sip and then began to cough. What the hell is this horrid vanilla taste? Did you put creamer in it or something?"

Mak began to chuckle. "That's the stuff in your feeding tube," he said. "I put it in since you wouldn't be able to feed yourself until your shoulder heals some and you start physical therapy."

"Oh, hell," Callie said and let her head fall back onto the pillow. "Not more physical therapy."

"Maybe it's time you thought about that fancy prosthetic the company was talking to you about," Mak said.

Callie rolled her eyes. "That thing was experimental and cost a small fortune."

"Maybe," Mak said with a shrug, "but new devices have to be tested somewhere and I thought that company you worked for over there was gonna pick up the big price tag."

"I'll think about it," she said as Rowdy wiped coffee from her chin.

Callie lifted her stump. "I suppose having a plastic and metal hand would be better than having no hand at all."

Rowdy kissed her. "You're gonna need two hands to hold our baby."

Callie snorted, "And feed it, change dirty diapers, and everything else." She said with a sigh. "I know Zena would help, but —"

"But Zena's gonna be taking care of a baby of her own. It wouldn't be right for you to saddle her with ours as well. I'm sure I can handle diapering, feeding, and other such chores." Rowdy bent and kissed her again. "I love you," he whispered, "and I'll do whatever it takes to make you happy, Miss Miller."

Callie stared up into his brown eyes and knew he was telling her the truth. He loved her with all her flaws, emotional wounds, and physical defects. He loved her; not Miller Ranch and its fat bank account—he loved her. She wanted to touch his stubbled cheek, but her shoulder hurt too much.

"And I love you, Mr. Waters," she said with tears in her eyes.

"So, what do you say to a nice harvest-themed wedding," Rowdy asked with a grin, "here on the Ranch with everything done up in reds, oranges, and yellows?"

Callie smiled. "We could serve cold cider rather than Champaign, and all the appetizers could be themed around turkey and pumpkin."

"How are you feeling, sweetie?" Sherri asked as she came into the room, holding Nathan's hand.

"Sore, but alive thanks to you, Mrs. Waters," Callie said as she accepted a kiss on the forehead from Sherri.

"Please call me Sherri. I was never Mrs. anybody," she said with a wink at her son, "and I'm perfectly fine with that. I always have been. It was everybody else in Jackson who had their panties in a twist because I had a kid without a husband."

"Well, Callie's not gonna do the same. We were just sitting here making plans for our wedding on the Ranch."

EPILOGUE

On the ninth of March, Rowdy and Callie Waters welcomed Caleb Miller Waters into the world.

"Will you look at that mess of red hair on that boy," Sherri Clearwater said to her new husband Nathan as they stood looking at the newborn through the glass window.

Nathan chuckled deep in his chest. "I'm sure he and Micah Jackson will have the run of that ranch by the time they can walk."

"And I'm sure you'll have the both of them on horseback long before then."

"They'll both be trained in the ways of the Cheyenne warrior, as they should be," he said with his chest puffed out in pride.

Sherri giggled as she rested her head on Nathan's arm. "You will teach them to be Indians while Cody and Callie teach them to be cowboys. The poor darlings are going to be so confused when they watch the old Westerns on television. They won't know which side to root for."

Nathan snorted. "They'll know," he said as they walked back toward Callie's room. "I just never knew this grandpa business was going to be so time-consuming."

Sherri wrapped her arms around her son's neck. "He's beautiful," she said, fighting back tears, "and I love the name Caleb." She walked over and planted a kiss on her daughter-in-law's forehead. "How are you feeling, Callie?"

"Like I could sleep for a week," she said with a yawn.

"Well, sleep all you can in here," Sherri said, "because when you get back home it's gonna be all about that little fella twenty-four/seven."

"I know," Callie said, lifting her prosthetic hand and flexing the robotic fingers, "it's why I brought this thing with me, so I could practice putting a diaper on him before we went home."

Sherri shook her head. "I still can't get over that thing. It's like science fiction come true or something."

"It took a little getting used to," Callie said, flexing the fingers again, "but yah, it's certainly a miracle and I'll be able to do so much more with the baby now."

"And your shoulder?" Sherri asked. "How's that doing after thirteen hours of labor?"

"Aching like a son-of-a-bitch," she said, "but getting more functional every day."

Sherri smiled. "That's great. What's your PT schedule going to be now that the baby is here?"

"Brenda will be coming out to work with me every day for a week or so after we get home and then we'll go back to two or three days a week."

"And what about Doris Jones's trial?" Nathan asked. "Will you be attending every day?"

"You bet she will," Rowdy said. "We want to see that sour old cow get what's coming to her."

"You're not worried some people are going to feel sorry for her," Sherri said, "and think she was just trying to get revenge for her son?"

"That won't hold up," Rowdy said, "because I'm the one

who killed Lucas, not Callie. So why'd she shoot Callie and not me?"

A nurse walked in carrying the baby for Callie to feed. "Didn't you hear the news?" the nurse asked. "Doris Jones accepted a plea and then had a massive stroke and died."

"Oh, my lord," Sherri gasped. "Well, at least it's all done and over with and you can all go home and not worry about some senile old crone shooting you through the damned window."

Callie held her new infant son close as the nurse opened her gown so she could nurse him. She stared down into his perfect pink face and her heart filled with a love she'd never expected.

Tears welled in her eyes as Rowdy joined her on the bed. "He looks just like you.

"Just that hair," Callie said, "but he has your eyes and mouth I think."

Rowdy kissed her forehead as Caleb began to nurse greedily. "I love you, Mrs. Waters."

"And I love you, Mr. Waters," she said as their lips touched.

Dear reader,

We hope you enjoyed reading *Sateside*. Please take a moment to leave a review, even if it's a short one. Your opinion is important to us.

Discover more books by Lori Beasley Bradley at
https://www.nextchapter.pub/authors/lori-beasley-bradley

Want to know when one of our books is free or discounted?
Join the newsletter at
http://eepurl.com/bqqB3H

Best regards,

Lori Beasley Bradley and the Next Chapter Team

You might also like:
Bad Moon Rising by Lori Beasley Bradley

To read the first chapter for free, please head to:
https://www.nextchapter.pub/books/bad-moon-rising

Stateside
ISBN: 978-4-82411-455-6

Published by
Next Chapter
1-60-20 Minami-Otsuka
170-0005 Toshima-Ku, Tokyo
+818035793528

13th November 2021

CPSIA information can be obtained
at www.ICGtesting.com
Printed in the USA
LVHW090448301121
704812LV00004B/399